THE SEVENTH SHADE

by

David Paul Bishop

Copyright © 2022, David Paul Bishop
Front cover created with Canva by David Paul Bishop.
All rights reserved.

I would like to dedicate this book to my friend, Mark, who looked in on me while I was recovering from hip surgery and without whose encouragement I might have given up on this work altogether.

Thank you, Mark.

There is a good chance that this book would have never existed without you.

Once upon a time, I, Zhuang Zhou, dreamed I was a butterfly, fluttering here and there, to all intents and purposes a butterfly. I was conscious only of my happiness as a butterfly, unaware that I was Zhou. Soon I awakened, and there I was, truly myself again. Now I do not know whether I was then a man dreaming I was a butterfly, or whether I am now a butterfly, dreaming I am a man.

— Zhuang Zhou, *The Zhuangzi*

Part One
Spheres of Torment

I think that the human mind, far from being a curse, is the most merciful thing in the world. We live on a quiet, sheltered island of ignorance, and from the single current flowing by our shores we visualize the vastness of the black seas around us, and see— simplicity and safety. And yet, if only a portion of the cross-currents and whirling vortices of mystery and chaos would be revealed to our consciousness, we should immediately go insane.

— Mearle Prout, *The House of the Worm*

Chapter One
The Doctors of Devland

"There's the exit for Cordele!"

His father's words contained a hint of excitement that pulled Corbin halfway out of his bored stupor. They had been on the road for nearly thirteen hours, and the droning of the Jeep's engine and the staticky rumble of the classic rock station his parents were listening to had begun to eclipse his memories of anything prior.

"That means we're almost there," James went on, his blue eyes sparkling at Corbin in the rearview mirror. "The exit for Devland is just a few miles south of Cordele."

It was a sweltering Monday afternoon in mid-July. The Georgia sun was a harsh white orb in a milky sea of what was more humidity than cloud-cover, and the cars on the interstate appeared to vibrate as they passed through shimmering heat mirages. Corbin closed one eye, attempting to line up a speck on his window with an oncoming car, imagining that he was aligning the sights of an antiaircraft gun. The blue Honda Civic raced past them, but not before Corbin drew a bead on it and clucked his tongue in unison, signaling the destruction of the enemy and the further survival of his imagined air base.

Corbin's mother, Emily, turned and looked at James, her green eyes squinting against the glare of the sun. She, like Corbin, had dark hair, a swarthy complexion, and a round face that stood in stark contrast to his father's angular features, fair skin, and shortly-cropped golden hair.

"Do you think we should stop and get something to eat before we get there?" she suggested.

James's mouth tightened, turning his elated smile into an unpleasant smirk.

"We have plenty of food to eat at home, Em," he said in a long-suffering, almost parental tone. "We're almost there. We can't be more than ten or fifteen minutes out now."

"Well, we're not going to the house, are we?" Emily reminded him curtly. "We still have to stop by your brother's first, unless the plan changed and nobody bothered to tell me about it."

"We won't be there for long," James replied dismissively. "Don't forget, it's going to be nearly two weeks before I see my first paycheck down here. We've got more pressing expenses to worry about than stopping for snacks every couple of hours."

"It's cute," Emily said in her calmest, most dangerous tone of voice, "when you get worked up about how I decide to spend *my* money."

Corbin sat with his head pressed against the window, scarcely daring to breathe. He wished that his mother had not brought up the subject of money. He was certain that his parents were about to start fighting again and that the fresh start that had been dangled in front of them was about to be snatched away.

For a long while, James simply stared straight ahead with his lips pressed tightly together. Then his features relaxed and he put on a thin smile.

"Yeah," he conceded. "Yeah, that's a fair point. After I start the new job and become the breadwinner of the family, you be sure to extend me the same courtesy. When I pull into the driveway some random evening with a keg of beer, a model airplane, and a llama, I don't want to hear a word out of you."

Emily gave him a smile that was barely more sincere than his own.

"You would do something crazy like that."

"Nah, not really," James said, his grin becoming broader and more genuine. "I promise you, Em: when I decide to purchase a llama, I will let you know so you can help me pick one."

Less than a minute later, they had taken the exit onto Margo Street. A green sign by the side of the road told Corbin that they still had a three-mile drive before they reached Devland, the town in which James had spent the first ten years of his life. James rarely talked about his childhood, assuring Corbin that some stories were best left untold, but he had let a few things slip over the years. Corbin did not have many details, but he knew that his father, his uncle, and his grandmother had been forced to flee Devland to escape the wrath of the man who served as the villain in most of his father's stories: Corbin's grandfather, Augustus Wendell.

Once they had reached the edge of the town, they stopped at a small restaurant and gas station called "Clair's General Store and Deli." All three of them decided on strawberry shortcake ice cream bars from a chilled bin beside the checkout counter, and Emily walked up to the register to pay.

"Will there be anything else?" the red-haired, pimply faced boy behind the counter asked dully. The nearly automatic manner in which he spoke led Corbin to believe that the question was merely a well-rehearsed mantra, the actual meaning of which had become lost over many years of vain repetitions.

"A pack ... of Marlboro Blacks?" James asked hopefully. Emily glanced over her shoulder at him, her face screwed up into a grimace of such blatant disapproval that he was quick to correct himself: "No, no; just the ice cream, thank you."

The pimply-faced boy had started to turn toward the rack of tobacco products behind him. He stopped himself, regarded the three of them with a look that betrayed his annoyance, and finalized their purchase at the register.

The heat of the summer sun pressed down upon Corbin and stung his eyes as he stepped out of the small convenience store. As he walked back toward the car and hastened to unwrap his ice cream bar, he heard his father mutter:

"You're really cracking the whip these days. Not even to celebrate the move, huh?"

"The move," Emily reminded him, "is why you've got to see this through. How many times have you quit smoking for a few days, and then decided to buy 'just one more pack' and quit later?"

James nodded in evident acceptance.

"We're starting our lives over," he agreed as they got into the car. "If I can't bring myself to quit now, when will I ever?"

"Exactly."

James let out a groan as he started up the engine.

"You just have no idea how rough it can be sometimes."

Corbin sullenly gazed at the reflection of his father's eyes in the rearview mirror. He could not remember a time in his life when his father had not smoked. He understood that it was bad for his father's health, but he had always felt like he understood why his father did it. Corbin had a habit of chewing his fingernails. Sometimes he would chew them so vigorously that he would make them bleed, but he could never bring himself to stop. In any case, Corbin had been trying harder than usual to curb his nail-biting tendencies, somehow believing that if he conquered his own habit, it would make it easier for his father to do the same.

"Hey," Emily said with a grin and punched James on the arm. "You got this, Doc! After all the mountains you've climbed and dragons you've slain to get here, riding out a bit of nicotine withdrawal should be no problem for an old legend like you."

Corbin knew that both of his parents had overcome many challenges and financial struggles on the road to his father's becoming a certified family physician. As far back as he could remember, his father had either been in school, working as an intern, or undergoing years of residency training. Most of the time, they had relied entirely on his mother's income as a retail worker at a number of different clothing and shoe outlets, and during the residency training, his father's wages had been meager at best.

There had been many nights when James and Emily's struggles had become too much for them to bear. Corbin had lain awake on those nights, listened to them as they spewed out their pent-up frustrations and anger at one another, feeling sickened and afraid that the life he knew was on the verge of falling apart.

In the end, however, they had managed to see it through. James finally had his certification in family medicine, and his brother, Kurt, had eagerly offered him a position at Doctor Wendell's Family Healthcare in Devland, Georgia. Emily had put in her last week at the shoe store in Morgantown, and James had used a U-Haul to move most of their belongings to the new house that they were going to be renting from his brother. At last, the three of them were on their way to start a new, better, long-awaited life.

"That's the elementary school I went to!" James pointed out a one-story, brick-walled building complex off to their left set back beyond a track, a ballfield, and a weathered playground. "A bit farther ahead, you can see the high school. The middle school you'll be going to this fall is part of that same building, over on the far side of it."

The high school complex was of a Brutalist architectural design that was rather similar to the elementary school, albeit a story taller. Corbin bit down on the now bare stick from his strawberry shortcake bar, a cold feeling settling in his gut. Making friends at his old school had been difficult, and he found the prospect of starting over to be a daunting one.

A few minutes after they had passed the school, a small, one-story movie theater came into view. A large red-and-gold metal plaque over the door identified the establishment as "The Devland Picture Palace," and a small marquee announced that it was currently showing two movies: *Oz the Great and Powerful* and *Texas Chainsaw 3D*.

Corbin was a bit underwhelmed by the fact that the self-proclaimed palace only appeared to be showing two movies, both of which had already come and gone in Morgantown theaters some months ago. He had seen a few of the TV spots for *Texas Chainsaw* and began to wonder if he might be able to talk his parents into taking him to see it, though he thought that he might have a better chance of selling them on the *Oz* movie.

As they drove further into Devland and the street came to be flanked by unbroken rows of townhouses, Corbin could not help but wonder if his grandfather lived in one of them. Corbin had only seen him once, so far as he knew. He had a vague recollection of his grandfather having been at one of his birthday parties, though the only impression that Corbin had retained of him was of his sharp, crystalline blue eyes. The rest of his face had been reduced to an ethereal gray fog with a grinning crack where a mouth ought to have been.

Corbin wondered whether, if he were to catch a glimpse of his grandfather's face peering out of one of the townhouse windows, they would recognize each other. He wondered if his grandfather even knew that they were coming to Devland, but he knew better than to ask. His parents were happier than they had been in a long time, and he did not want to risk ruining that by asking awkward questions.

James turned right off of Margo Street onto Foxglove Lane. Less than a minute later, house number one hundred twenty-four, where Corbin's uncle Kurt lived, came up on their left. There was a garage attached to the right side of the house with enough room for them to park alongside Uncle Kurt's silver Buick Enclave, but James stopped short of the garage, opting to park in the shade of a gangly Virginia pine instead.

The house was three stories tall, and it seemed to Corbin as if it were the best-kept out of all of the ones they had driven by thus far. Its white paint was clean and unchipped, and the trim appeared to be brand-new. In front of the house and running alongside the garage were eight English boxwoods in freshly mulched beds, each of them trimmed to symmetrical perfection.

Corbin followed his parents down the cobblestone path toward the front door. He had a faint recollection of having met Uncle Kurt once, many years ago, and there had not been a birthday in his entire life when Corbin had failed to receive a card from him. He understood that his uncle would ordinarily have been at work on Mondays, but he had taken the day off so that he could be there to meet them when they arrived.

"Jimmy!" Uncle Kurt greeted his brother at the door with a broad smile on his round face. He was attired in jean shorts and a white polo shirt, and the hair on his head was black and thick like ravens' feathers. He had a well-groomed mustache, his eyes were dark brown and gleaming, and his whole face had an excited glow about it.

James extended his arm but, rather than merely taking his hand, Uncle Kurt pulled him into a hug. For a moment, the gesture appeared to have caught James off guard, but at length he returned the embrace. Uncle Kurt went on to hug Emily as well, and then he placed a hand on Corbin's shoulder and regarded him warmly.

"Well, look how you've grown!" he exclaimed. "Last time I saw you, you weren't more than knee-high to a grasshopper, running around with a mason jar trying to catch lightning bugs!"

Uncle Kurt proceeded to wrap him in his arms, and Corbin put an uncomfortable arm around him as well. Corbin wanted to like his uncle, and he had no reason as of yet to dislike him, but he found his uncle's overt display of affection, as well as his vague reference to some long-forgotten lightning bug hunt, to be a bit overwhelming.

"Sometime," Uncle Kurt addressed James, motioning toward Corbin with a nod of his head, "I've got to take this young man out onto Lake Blackshear for some fishing and to get to know him properly. You remember the lake, right?"

"We made some good memories out there," James said with a grin. This reaction surprised Corbin, who was unused to seeing his father looking back on that period in his life with any measure of fondness. Noticing Corbin's questioning stare and seemingly misinterpreting it, James elaborated: "Blackshear is an artificial lake where your grandparents used to take us fishing."

Corbin smiled and nodded in acknowledgement, though the thought of his father, uncle, and grandparents going boating, fishing, or doing most anything else together made him uncomfortable. His whole life, he had perceived his grandfather as an enigmatic and grotesque entity, and he found it difficult to imagine him passing as an ordinary father taking his kids on a trip to the lake.

"Good heavens," Uncle Kurt cried with a level of exuberance that reminded Corbin of a child on Christmas morning, "this is all so exciting! It's so good to have all of you here. And I'm so proud of you, Jimmy! I know that you know that—God knows I've told you enough times over the phone—but I am so happy that you went through with this."

"I'm glad it worked out too," James said, his casual poise strikingly contrasted against Uncle Kurt's buoyant mirth. "I really appreciate you giving me this opportunity. I'm not sure if I thanked you properly over the phone. I was just too overwhelmed to find the right words for it at the time."

"No, my boy," Uncle Kurt corrected him, "thank *you*. I am getting on toward being an old man. I need a younger, stronger partner who is willing to carry more than his fair share of the load."

"Not that much older than me. And I hope you won't be giving this young, strong partner too much more than his fair share. I'm still a novice. You're not going to try to run me into the ground on my first week, are you?"

"Of course, you're a novice! That's what makes you such an ideal candidate for the position. You're a hapless newbie and haven't the first clue what your fair share is."

"That's fair enough."

"Well, why are you all standing at the door like you came here to sell me a vacuum cleaner? Come in! Come in and make yourselves at home."

Uncle Kurt escorted them into a spacious parlor, practically shooing them toward a red leather sofa facing a fifty-eight-inch television that was mounted over a stonework fireplace. James seated himself on the far end, Emily placed herself on the opposite side, and Corbin sat down between them.

"Would you like a beer?" Uncle Kurt asked James. "I usually drink a glass of wine in the evening, but I figured you would be more of a beer-drinking type, so I stocked a few bottles in the fridge."

James began to massage his right wrist with his left hand. It seemed to Corbin as if his father were doing so for no other reason than to bring his arms across his front, as if he were feeling threatened or attacked, though his face betrayed no sign of discomfort.

"You pegged me correctly," James said. He glanced across Corbin toward Emily and, seemingly not picking up on any objection from her, added: "Yes, a beer would be nice!"

"For you, Em?" Uncle Kurt asked. "A beer? Or perhaps a glass of sauvignon blanc?"

She smiled at him and shook her head.

"And you, Cory?" he went on, smiling at Corbin. "I have Pepsi and Sprite, if you'd like one."

Corbin stared at his uncle, mortified. He had only just found it in his heart to forgive his uncle for the uninvited embrace with which he had been greeted at the door, and he felt that this unabashed use of the moniker "Cory" had just taken their relationship back to square one.

"We haven't called him 'Cory' since he was a baby," James broke the silence. "You don't remember that, do you, Corbin?"

"I don't," Corbin replied in a deceptively cheerful tone. "A Sprite would be nice! Thank you, Uncle Kurt."

Uncle Kurt nodded at him with a blissfully ignorant smile and disappeared through a door on his right.

"You know, James," Uncle Kurt called out from the next room, "Mom is proud of you too. I probably should have let you break the news to her yourself, but what can I say? I was too excited to restrain myself from shouting it from the rooftops, as it were, and I have full confidence in your ability to forgive me for that. You've spoken to her since I spilled that particular can of beans, I am sure?"

"Of course," James said.

"When she first found out," Uncle Kurt went on, "she was so happy that I thought she was going to burst! She did that thing she does when she gets excited. You know, where she starts repeating herself and the whole conversation starts going around in circles?"

"Yeah," James said with a slight smile, "I know what you mean."

"Well, in this case, it was, 'I'm so proud of him! I'm so proud of my little boy,' " Uncle Kurt's voice cracked as he attempted to imitate her, "that she was repeating. You know, you did have us scared for a little while there."

Corbin could physically feel the uneasiness that fell over the room. His father seemed to bristle and go rigid. His mother's arm twitched as if she wanted to lay a comforting hand on him, and Corbin wished he had not sat down between them so that she could more readily do so. James's muscles began to relax, however, and he merely replied:

"Yeah, well, I sort of scared myself for a while there too."

Uncle Kurt returned with a stemware glass, a bottle of shiraz wine, a freshly opened bottle of Stella Artois, and Corbin's can of Sprite.

"But that's all behind us now!" His face beamed at James as he offered him the Stella Artois. "Everything is going to get better for us from here on out. Out of its ashes, the phoenix rises!"

Corbin knew that, on the occasions when his father drank, he preferred Budweiser, and it seemed to him as if he were regarding the bottle that Uncle Kurt was offering him with a rather dubious eye. James took it with a smile, regardless.

"Thank you," James said. "And, yes, the phoenix hopes to do a lot better from here on out."

Corbin took his can of Sprite with a polite "Thank you." He took a sip, and the beverage felt cold, refreshing, and bubbly on the roof of his mouth. He watched his uncle move toward a leather chair off to the left of the stonework fireplace and sit down.

"I do enjoy a glass of wine now and then," Uncle Kurt said, dividing his attention between James and the wine that he was pouring into his glass. "It helps me relax, and I firmly believe that a little fruit of the vine does more good than it does harm. But never more than a glass, mind you! I am on call twenty-four-seven. At any moment, the pager that lives on my hip could start screaming at me, and whenever that happens, I have to be sober enough to take a trip to the Anderson Memorial emergency room."

"Ah, yes," James said with a laugh. "The General Robert H. Anderson Memorial Hospital. I still remember when Mom had to take me there, right after Dad nearly beat the life out of me."

Corbin sat up a little straighter. His father had rarely spoken about the events of that night, and Corbin hoped that he was about to be given a chance to fill in some of the gaps in the narrative. He noticed that a disturbed expression had crept over Uncle Kurt's face.

"How much do you remember about that night?" Uncle Kurt asked.

To Corbin's disappointment, his father merely said: "Not much. I remember that I didn't enjoy my stay at the hospital. It was a house of horrors. Seemed like there were more interns looking to prove their worth than there were real doctors. I felt like a lab rat in a second-rate classroom."

"Well, what did you expect, Jimmy?" Uncle Kurt said with a smile that Corbin found difficult to read. "Welcome to Devland."

"Home sweet home," James sighed disdainfully.

"No heavy drinking," Uncle Kurt picked up where he had left off, "and absolutely never any drinking in public. While you are in my employ, I must insist that this rule apply to you as well. No wild nights out on the town. As practitioners of medicine, it wouldn't do to have the people that place such faith in our medical advice seeing us subjecting our livers to the evils of alcohol."

It occurred to Corbin that his uncle had offered his father a beer for no other reason than that it gave him an excuse to segue into this well-rehearsed monologue on the evils of alcohol. The realization that their beverages had been offered to them to serve a means rather than out of generosity made him appreciate his Sprite a little less.

"Or," James replied, "to have them catch us reaping the benefits of an occasional glass of the fruit of the vine?"

"Correct," Uncle Kurt said. "If someone were to walk into a bar and spy me indulging in a glass, they would have no way of knowing if it was my first glass or my ninth, and the last thing that my practice needs is to have people spreading rumors about me. This is a small town, and news travels fast. If you break wind in the street, the whole town hears about it before you smell it yourself. On a similar note, you have given up smoking by now, haven't you?"

"Absolutely," James said. "That's behind me now."

Corbin noted that his father did not bother to mention how close behind him it was.

"I am glad to hear that," Uncle Kurt said with a smile of approval. "How we present ourselves to our patients is of the utmost importance. To expect them to live in accordance with our medical advice while we smoke cigarettes and booze it up would be the very definition of doing a Conway."

Corbin had never heard the expression "doing a Conway" before, but he felt that he understood the gist of it, and he saw his father nodding his head in evident agreement.

"It hasn't been easy," Uncle Kurt went on, "getting my practice established and gaining the trust of the people in this town. The Wendell name has developed something of an unsavory reputation here, as I'm sure you can understand."

"I can imagine," James grunted. "How is the old man doing these days anyway?"

"Father is doing all right. He's been staying in a trailer on the west side of town, complaining about a supposedly chronic back injury and living off of the generosity of the state of Georgia. He trades with the other folks in the trailer park, exchanging leftover food stamps for cash and illicit prescription drugs, and aside from that, he seldom leaves his trailer. His life is in ruins, by my way of reckoning, but you don't have to worry about him. He has all that he needs to get by for whatever is left of his life."

"Yeah, that's about where I imagined the old parasite would be by now."

"Mom never saw him as a parasite," Uncle Kurt reminded him, his voice adopting a mildly scolding tone. "She always believed that he was just sick. It about broke her heart to leave him like that—then, when he needed us so much—but, all things considered, I don't suppose she had much of a choice."

"Of course, she didn't have a choice," James fervently agreed, and Corbin noticed that he was gripping the neck of his beer bottle so tightly that his fingers had started to turn white. "Not after what happened. Anyway, he didn't need us. That old man pushed us out of his life a long, long time before we gave up on him."

Uncle Kurt fell silent, seemingly having become preoccupied with the wine in his glass. He studied it for a while, carefully noting the way it swirled and sloshed as he rotated his wrist, before his face suddenly lit up and he started talking once more:

"Anyway, that's all in the past now, and a bright and beautiful future lies ahead of us! As it turns out, when it comes to starting over and forging new friendships here in Devland, a unique opportunity may have presented itself. I've been planning on having some friends over for a cookout this coming Sunday afternoon. Nothing formal; just pulling out the grill and cooking up some hotdogs and burgers with a few folks I know through work. As it turns out, you moved here just in time to be a part of the festivities! Some of the families there will have children close to Corbin's age. It'd give him a chance to make some connections before he starts attending the local school."

A tingle of excitement rose up inside Corbin. Making friends had never been his strong suit, and as nervous as the thought of this cookout made him, he readily welcomed the opportunity to forge an alliance or two before school started.

"What do you think, Em?" James asked.

"We just got into town," Emily replied hesitantly. "It'd be nice to take a few weeks to get settled in a bit before we start working on expanding our social circles. And Corbin doesn't do well with big events like that."

Corbin looked down at his Sprite in disappointment. Regardless of his feelings on the matter, socialization had become inevitable, and he had begun to relish the thought of dipping his toes into the town's waters a bit before plunging into their unknown depths.

"Well, he's got to outgrow that sometime!" Uncle Kurt discarded her concerns with a laugh. "And what better place for him to start than at a small, intimate gathering like a cookout?"

"Well, we *did* just get here," James backed Emily up. "Thank you for thinking of us, but I'm afraid we better pass this time."

Uncle Kurt's smile faltered, but the look in his eyes remained unchanged.

"If nothing else," he advised coolly, "think of coming to this cookout as a political maneuver. While I would like to see Corbin make some friends and get off on the right foot, at the very least, your coming will give a few of my patients a chance to connect a face to your name and help make them more comfortable with the thought of scheduling appointments with the new doctor in town."

Corbin smiled appreciatively at Uncle Kurt, knowing that he had just won the battle. James stole a glance at Emily, who shrugged in evident acceptance.

"Well, in that case," James said, "I'm sure we can make time for it."

"Excellent!" Uncle Kurt exclaimed, slapping his leg in jubilation. "I'll be expecting you here on Sunday at two o'clock. Now, Corbin, on a more serious note, there is something I have to ask you."

Uncle Kurt was looking directly at him, his face devoid of its previous joviality.

"You don't believe in ghosts, do you?"

Corbin stared back at his uncle, caught off guard by the sudden turn that the conversation had taken. After a moment of deathly silence, both of his parents began to laugh. It was not a mirthful laugh; it was the sort of laugh that they used when trying to make light of something that they did not want Corbin to worry about.

"He does not," James answered for him. "We raised him better than that."

Uncle Kurt smiled awkwardly.

"I'm sorry," he said. "It's just that…. Well, he's bound to hear about it eventually, isn't he? I thought it might be better for him to hear the truth of it before he gets caught off guard by one of the stories that they tell around here."

"The truth about what?" Corbin asked, but nobody looked at him.

"He'll hear all about it, in time, from us," James addressed Uncle Kurt stiffly. "We were hoping that he could spend a few nights in the house and get the chance to see it for what it is before anybody put any weird ideas in his head, but…. Well, I suppose it's really my fault, isn't it? I should have let you know where we were coming from."

"No, the fault is mine," Uncle Kurt admitted. "I shouldn't have taken it upon myself to bring it up."

Corbin glanced from his father to his uncle, then to his mother and back to his father. Not one of them met his eye, and a cold feeling of dread began to screw its way into his gut. He had never understood his parents' exasperating tendency to attempt to protect him by leaving him in the dark. At times such as these, he had nowhere to turn to for answers but his own imagination, and his imaginings were almost unfailingly grimmer than the truth.

After a few moments of uncomfortable silence, James tipped his beer to his lips and finished it in a large swallow. Picking up on this, Uncle Kurt got to his feet and said:

"I suppose you must be anxious to get to your new home after that beast of a drive you had."

"We really should be going," James concurred, standing up as well. The two brothers shook hands, pulling each other into a one-armed hug.

"Again," Uncle Kurt said, "I'm sorry I couldn't do any better with the housing. If there was anything else that I could have done—"

"Forget it," James cut him off. "It's not a problem. Like I said: we didn't raise Corbin to believe in ghosts."

Uncle Kurt's reply came in a whisper that Corbin could barely make out:

"You know it's not the ghost stories that've got me worried, Jimmy."

James, Emily, and Corbin proceeded to say their goodbyes and make their way back toward the front door. There were handshakes and hugs and many amiably spoken words of farewell, but Corbin noticed that, through it all, his father never once met Uncle Kurt's eyes.

Chapter Two
The Seeds of Madness

"That's where I'll be working with your uncle," James told Corbin, indicating a renovated two-story townhouse coming up on their right. Corbin saw that there was a white wooden sign in the front lawn that read *Doctor Wendell's Family Healthcare.* It looked as if there was a rather spacious parking lot behind the townhouse.

"Normally, Uncle Kurt would be at work today," James went on. "He left the practice in the hands of his partner, Doctor Goodman, so he could be at home when we got into town. There's also Joshua, a young fellow. He's not a doctor, but he helps to keep the place tidy and does whatever else Uncle Kurt needs him to do. And there's Missus Sherman. She answers the phone and makes all of the appointments."

"And, starting tomorrow," Emily added with a grin, "there's you! The other Doctor Wendell. Are they going to change the sign to reflect that? Shouldn't it say 'Doctors Wendell?' Or 'Doctor Wendells's?' "

" '*Wendells's,*' " James repeated under his breath. "Don't be silly. The second 'Wendell' is silent, just like the second 'l' at the end of it and the 'Goodman' in the middle."

"Wendel-ul." Emily added the extra "l" sound to their name thoughtfully, seeming to roll it around in her mouth as if she was trying to decide whether she liked the taste of it or not. "Or it could be 'Wendy,' if you follow the rule in Spanish where the double 'l' makes a 'y' sound. You should add a disclaimer to the sign, letting people know that you don't sell burgers and Frosties."

"Oh, sure!" James heartily agreed. "I'll just sneak back here tonight with a can of spray paint and make the necessary changes. Won't Kurt be surprised?"

James and Emily laughed, and Corbin tightly closed his eyes in an effort to shut out the sounds of their deceptive revelry. A dark cloud had settled over the three of them, and he found his parents' pretentious cheeriness to be more insulting than it was comforting.

They turned right onto Butterwort Street. Corbin recalled his father having mentioned that the house was on Butterwort Street; number one hundred and twenty-one, if he remembered correctly.

"Of course," James went on, "there are advantages to leaving the sign the way it is. It might be good for business to have people wandering in like: 'Hello, can I get a burger and fries?' 'No, but, since you're here, can we put you down for a flu shot and a colonoscopy?' "

"Why is Uncle Kurt scared of the house we're moving into?"

The question spilled out of Corbin in a moment of insurmountable frustration, and he immediately regretted it. He was sure that his father was about to start shouting at him, but James answered quite calmly:

"The house has been empty for a long time, and it has come to have something of a bad reputation. People like to tell stories about it being haunted, and it has become something of a rite of passage for young people in Devland to dare each other to break in and spend the night there."

James shot Emily a questioning look, seemingly uncertain of how much he should say. He seemed to interpret her silence as permission to proceed, so he went on:

"There's a fair number of folks that swear they've seen and heard things lurking in the old house on Butterwort Street. The most commonly told of these stories is one about a man named Diggory Fallon. When he was about sixteen years old, he claimed to have spent a night in the house, and he came out the next day raving about ghosts and goblins and whatever else goes bump in the night. Not long after that, he was committed to the Anderson Memorial psychiatric ward, and he's been in and out of various institutions ever since."

Corbin felt a thrill of horror beginning to creep up his spine.

"The house made him go crazy?" he asked.

"Not at all," James said firmly. "The Fallon boy was unstable to begin with. The madness was already there, growing inside of him. The house, together with his own expectations about it, were merely the straws that broke the camel's back. But people do love a good ghost story, and when you start going to school, you're liable to hear all sorts of strange things about the Fallon boy and the old Wendell house. When it's all said and done, though, it's just a house, and there's nothing there that can hurt us. Do you understand, Corbin?"

"I understand," Corbin said, though he felt as if his father had not been completely honest with him.

It's not the ghost stories that've got me worried, Uncle Kurt had said.

A mailbox appeared on their left with the number one hundred and twenty-one stickered to the side of it. They pulled into the driveway, and Corbin found himself looking up at his father's first childhood home. Immediately, his spirits rose. After his uncle's dire warnings, he had come to expect that the house was going to be dark and gloomy and that the very sight of it would instill him with a sense of dread. He was pleasantly surprised to find that, though it may have been old and the white paint on the walls had started to peel, his first impression of the two-story house was that it looked like a comfortable place to live.

James parked the car, and the three of them stepped out into the summer heat. Gravel flecked with resilient weeds crunched beneath their shoes as they approached a small wooden porch.

Corbin watched as his father put an arm around Emily's waist and stooped down in an evident effort to sweep her legs out from beneath her. His mother nearly toppled over before she managed to shove him off of her with an alarmed squeal.

"What are you doing?!" she cried.

"I'm trying to carry my bride across the threshold," James replied, seemingly startled by her resistance to his efforts. "It's tradition!"

James's face bore an innocent smile, though his hands had started to grasp at Emily in ways that seemed to have little to do with finding her center of balance. She laughed and leaned her weight into his shoulder for a moment, but then she smacked at his arm and gave him another shove backward.

"You frisky schoolboy!" she chided him. "If you want to carry something across the threshold, why don't you start by carrying a few of those boxes?"

"As you wish," James consented with a heavy sigh. "You mind lending a hand, Corbin?"

James opened the trunk and handed the keys to Emily, and he and Corbin both picked up a box and followed her down the stone walkway toward the front of the house. The small wooden porch creaked under their weight as Emily inserted the key into a deadbolt which seemed to turn with some difficulty, and then the two of them followed her into a small, sweltering room.

The room was closed off from the rest of the house and appeared to have served as a stopping point where one had the chance to remove their shoes. Over on their left, against one of the lime green walls, was a wooden bench with red, weathered cushions. The hardwood floor directly in front of the bench was in perfect condition, suggesting that there had once been a rug there so that people could sit down on the bench, take off their shoes, and avoid tracking mud and snow directly onto the floor. Farther away from the bench, the hardwood was scuffed and gritty, suggesting to Corbin that people had more often than not failed to utilize the rug. James and Corbin set their boxes down on the bench and followed Emily through another door, none of them bothering to remove their shoes.

    Upon passing through the doorway, they found themselves in a comfortable-looking living room with a well-stuffed chair, a couch, and their old television sitting on top of a small cabinet in the far-right corner. Corbin was pleased to notice that the house beyond the mudroom was much cooler. He heard the hum of a window air conditioning unit coming from somewhere around the corner on his left, and he was grateful that his father had possessed the foresight to leave it turned on over the weekend.

    "All aboard for the grand tour!" James called out exuberantly. He led them through the doorway on their left into what appeared to be a sitting room. There were two couches facing each other, and beyond them, Corbin saw four shelves full of dust-covered books. He eyed the small library with piqued interest, making a mental note that he was going to have to go over them with a more attentive eye after the tour was over. On their right was an open doorway that led into what looked like a bathroom. Corbin recognized the supreme importance of this discovery, and he made a mental note of its location as well.

    James next led them through another doorway into a dining room, and Corbin saw that the air conditioner he had heard since exiting the mudroom was set up in a window on his right. The room was equipped with a table and six wooden chairs, four of which looked as if they were supposed to have been part of a set along with the table. Past the table was a trapdoor which Corbin assumed led to a basement. On his left was another doorway, and he peered through it long enough to observe a kitchen equipped with a stove, an oven, a toaster, the microwave and coffee percolator from their old apartment, and a refrigerator with a small, vertical freezer built into the side of it.

Corbin turned away from the kitchen and began to follow his parents up a staircase. When they reached the top, they headed off to the right, made a one hundred and eighty degree turn, and stepped forward into an unpleasantly warm hallway that ran off to their left.

"This is our room," James addressed Emily with a grin, indicating a red-stained wooden door directly in front of them. He opened the door, and a draft of cool air from another window air conditioning unit rolled over Corbin's face as he took in the sight of pale blue walls and a neatly-made bed with two white pillows and a burgundy comforter. It occurred to Corbin that this might have been the bed upon which his father and uncle had been conceived, and the thought made him so uncomfortable that he decided to fix his attention on the hallway's fine hardwood flooring instead.

James shut the bedroom door and began to lead them farther down the hall. Directly ahead of them, Corbin spied a pulldown door with a short length of rope hanging off of it.

"Is there an attic?" he asked, indicating the dangling rope.

"There is," James confirmed.

"What's up there?"

"Nothing. Just rafters and empty space."

Corbin remained transfixed by the pulldown door. He had lived in apartments his whole life and, while he was familiar with the concept of attics from movies and books, he had never actually been in one before. At length, James asked:

"Do you want to take a look?"

Corbin nodded eagerly. James stepped around him and pulled the rope, releasing a set of spring-loaded folding steps. No sooner had he unfolded the steps than Corbin hastened to ascend them. A nearly overwhelming wave of heat came cascading down to meet him, and his eyes began to smart as he stuck his head and shoulders up into the oppressive flow of air. He peered into the darkness just long enough to observe a peaked ceiling, rafters, and bare plywood flooring, and then he came scurrying back down.

"Close it," Corbin implored his father. "You're letting all the heat in!"

James chuckled as he folded the stairs back into the ceiling, and then he led the way to a doorway on their left. Beyond it was a large room with a single leather chair, a coffee table, and three shelves full of books.

"This was my father's domain," James told them, and it seemed to Corbin that his voice held an edge of contempt. "He spent a lot of time in here, settled in with his books and a bottle of Jack Daniels."

Corbin noticed that his father seemed hesitant to get too close to the room and that he was quick to lead them away from it. Corbin saw that there was a bathroom at the hall's far end, and on their right were two more doors.

"This used to be your uncle Kurt's room," James addressed Corbin, indicating the first of the doors. "It's yours now."

James and Emily both held back, allowing Corbin the courtesy of opening the door himself. Upon doing so, he saw his old dresser, a twin bed in the left corner equipped with a green and blue patchwork quilt, an old and curling *Return of the Jedi* poster pinned to the wall on his right, a window air conditioning unit that was humming pleasantly in the far window, and a nightstand beside the bed that housed a lamp with a stained, yellowing shade and his old radio.

Corbin had used that radio's cassette deck to record many an albums' worth of early two thousand's rock over the years. He was glad to see that it, too, had made the move with them.

"Is that your old room?" Corbin asked, stepping back out into the hall and gesturing toward the last door before the bathroom.

"Yes," James said. "Want to see it?"

Corbin nodded, and James led them down the hall and opened the door. Upon stepping inside, Corbin took note of the fact that this was the smallest of the three bedrooms and that there was no air conditioning unit present. It contained a small bed, a nightstand with a twelve-inch-tall toy Tyrannosaurus and a brown lamp sitting on it, and an absurd-looking poster of a clown that had been thumbtacked to the wall facing the foot of the bed.

Though he could not readily say why, Corbin found the clown poster to be unsettling. Its white-painted face, cartoonishly oversized blue eyes, widely smiling mouth, and bulging, balloon-like polka dot suit all struck him as looking deformed rather than amusing. There was something else about the room—and, now that he thought about it, the whole house—that was beginning to set him on edge, though it took him a while to figure out precisely what it was.

The posters, he mused. *The toy T-Rex; the furniture; and so, so many books....*

It finally clicked in his mind: His grandparents had left the house with nothing but the bare essentials. They had not taken the time to bring anything heavy with them, like chairs or couches. They had not even bothered to roll up the posters on the walls or to pack up his father's toy Tyrannosaurus. Had they left in such a hurry, he wondered, because they had been running away from something? A feeling of unease began to settle over him, and he had to take a moment to reassure himself and to recall what his father had told him on the drive over: it was just a house, and all of the tales that people had come to tell about it were just ghost stories.

You know it's not the ghost stories that've got me worried....

James seemed to sense Corbin's unease, and he laughed and shook his head at the clown poster in evident embarrassment.

"Kind of spooky, isn't he?" James admitted. "When I was a kid, I thought he looked funny. Of course, that was before Stephen King went and turned clowns into something to be scared of."

Corbin shot his father a baleful look.

"Clowns aren't scary," he retorted. "But this one…. He looks like he had an allergic reaction to something."

James raised an eyebrow, and Emily guffawed loudly.

"Is this where your night terrors came from?" she asked with a laugh. "From a poster of a clown with seafood allergies?"

James's face began to redden.

"Well," he said, "if you have both finished taking a wet, steaming dump on my childhood—"

This remark merely made Emily laugh so hard that Corbin could not help but join in.

"If you are *quite* done," James began again, starting to show signs of genuine irritation, "there's still a lot of boxes left to bring inside. What do you say we get started?"

The three of them began to carry the last of their belongings into their new house. Corbin tried to estimate how many trips he was going to have to make. Four, if they all pitched in? Maybe five? Each time he passed through the mudroom, the heat and humidity that seemed to define the state of Georgia pressed down on him and took his breath away. Every time he made it back into the living room, a cool draft from the air conditioner played across the sweat on his face and offered a brief moment of respite.

On his third trip to the car, Corbin saw that two children were sitting on bicycles across the street from them. There was a bright-eyed girl of twelve or thirteen with long, golden locks of hair wearing a white crop top and jeans sitting astride a black Cannondale. Behind her was a dark-haired, lanky boy of about fourteen in a black T-shirt and blue jeans straddling a red Roubaix. They were both holding open backpacks in their laps and sipping water out of plastic bottles, discreetly conversing among themselves, but their eyes kept casting wary glances toward Corbin and the house.

Corbin had no doubt that their water break was a ruse. He was certain that they had chosen to park there because they were curious about the Wendell house and wanted an excuse to observe its new occupants. He was less offended by the realization that he was being spied on than he was by their lack of subtlety, and he made a deliberate effort not to look at them as he approached the Jeep.

Farther down Butterwort Street, at the point where it began to curve off to the left to meet up with Margo Street, Corbin caught sight of two more figures, still and silent like a pair of sentries. The first was a short, brawny boy of about fifteen with buzzed black hair and olive skin. He was wearing a gray tank top and sitting slouch-shouldered atop a white bike, seeming to regard both Corbin and the house with equal measures of disdain.

Just behind him on his left was a girl of eleven or twelve with straight black hair. She was dressed in a black sweatshirt and slacks and was straddling a silver bike with her arms across her chest. Her gaze passed back and forth between Corbin and the first two bikers, her expression betraying a measure of contempt. As for whether her disgust was directed toward the overt gawking of the other bikers or toward himself, Corbin could only guess.

He pulled the next box out of the back of the Jeep and turned toward the house. Feeling the eyes of the bikers upon him as he made his may down the gravel path, Corbin found himself starting to daydream about his own bike. He imagined himself riding through the backstreets of Devland, cruising at a speed where the wind on his face would evaporate his sweat, searching out whatever shops and secret places the little town might have to offer. For a moment, he even dared to imagine himself riding beside the four bikers he had just seen, accepted and surrounded by new friends.

After the last of the boxes had been brought in, Corbin took it upon himself to explore the house a little further. The first thing he did was check out the basement beneath the trapdoor, and it was there that he found his bike. The silver Gary Fisher Tiburon was leaning on its kickstand off to the right of the stairway.

Corbin brushed the tips of his fingers across the handlebars, wistfully recalling the sense of comfort that this machine had once brought him. Why had he stopped riding it? He had just lost interest in it, he supposed, but at that moment, for the first time in well over two years, the urge to hear the buzz of pavement beneath his tires and to feel the ache in his calves as he conquered hills burned within him like a fever. He was reluctant to admit to himself that this sudden urge had been brought on by the sight of the four bikers outside and by the prospect that he might happen upon them and be invited to ride with them.

They probably wouldn't want to ride with me anyway.

An unaccountable sense of melancholy began to wash over him, and he fought it off by busying his senses with the rest of the basement's contents. On his left, he saw a doorway atop a small flight of concrete steps that led up to their backyard. To the left of the doorway was a small window. Tiny shards of glass crunched beneath Corbin's shoes as he walked toward it. The window had been broken and replaced, he realized, and he began to think back to what his father had said about people daring each other to break into the old Wendell house.

He turned his back to the window. Against the wall on his left were a washing machine, a dryer, and a large chest freezer. Feeling curious, he lifted the freezer's lid, but he found that it was both empty and unplugged.

"Corbin?" Emily called to him from the top of the steps. "You down here?"

"Yes!" he called back to her, quietly dropping the top of the freezer back into place.

"You mind giving us a hand unpacking?"

The three of them spent the rest of the afternoon unpacking the last of their belongings, stocking the kitchen cabinets with pastas and other non-perishable items, and playfully bickering about where everything should go. There was a point in the process where James made a playful grab for Emily's backside. She fended him off with a rolled-up dish towel, chasing him halfway up the stairs before heeding his high-pitched cries for mercy, and Corbin felt a sense of tranquility that he had not known in years. They had made it. His father was about to start his new, long-awaited career, his parents were laughing and carrying on the way they used to, and at that moment, he had no doubt that everything was actually going to work out for them.

That evening, they sat down to a simple dinner of spaghetti, canned green beans, and toast. As he attempted to spread cold butter over his toast, Corbin asked his father:

"What time do you have to be at work?"

"Six o'clock," James replied through a mouthful of pasta. He swallowed hard before adding: "Somebody remind me to set the alarm clock for five. That should allow me plenty of time to get ready."

"I want to get up at five too," Corbin announced.

James glanced at Emily, evidently attempting to gauge her feelings on the matter. She merely sat with her fork halfway to her mouth, a bewildered expression on her face.

"Five o'clock is an awfully early start for a growing boy with no particular place to be," James answered hesitantly. "You'll be losing enough sleep when school starts. What would you want to wake at a five for anyway?"

"To see you off," Corbin said quietly, mindlessly prodding at his now tattered piece of toast.

James raised his eyebrows in amusement, and Emily smiled warmly and resumed eating.

"Well," James said with a laugh, "I'm going to try not to wake you tomorrow. But if you hear the alarm go off and you feel like getting out of bed, I'm not going to stop you from coming downstairs and having breakfast with me before I head out."

Corbin was satisfied with this answer. He had woken up to the sound of his parents' alarm clock countless times, and he had no doubt that he would do so again.

"Get a load of this guy," James said to Emily, his face beaming with pride.

"I think it's sweet," she quietly agreed, smiling back at him.

"Yeah, it'll be sweet while it lasts," James sighed, resuming the act of cutting his spaghetti down to a more manageable length. "Waking up at five a.m. isn't any fun, Corbin. If you hear that alarm going off tomorrow and you don't feel like getting up yet, you go ahead and fall back to sleep."

Corbin nodded. He did not bother to mention that one of the reasons he wanted to wake up at five was so that he might get an earlier start at riding his bike and, in so doing, increase his chances of coming across the bikers he had seen that afternoon.

That evening, the three of them sat down to watch a movie. They did not have cable yet, James explained, following up with a promise that he would have it taken care of tomorrow or the next day. They allowed Corbin to pick something to watch from their DVD collection, and he chose *The Woman in Black,* prompting his father to shake his head in dismay.

"I don't know where he gets it," James said. "If I watched half the movies he's into when I was his age, I'd have hidden under the blankets and never come out. I'd still be under a blanket, walking around like a sheet ghost. What kind of a medical practice would want a doctor like that?"

"What wife would want a husband like that?" Emily added.

James stared at her, a wounded expression on his face.

"I thought you liked me under the blankets," he said.

Emily groaned, rolled her eyes, and suppressed a laugh.

"Where did I ever find such an obnoxious man-child?"

"You just got lucky, I guess," James replied, grinning at her.

The three of them sat down and watched the movie together. Less than halfway through, they took a short break while Emily dished out bowls of chocolate ice cream for each of them, which they enjoyed with the remainder of *The Woman in Black*.

It was getting close to nine o'clock when the movie ended. James, Corbin, and Emily worked around each other to brush their teeth in the upstairs bathroom, and then Corbin changed into his rust-colored cotton pajamas and crawled under his quilt. It was warm enough that he did not need the quilt, but the weight of it gave him an unexplainable sense of comfort. He lay on his side, studying his uncle's *Return of the Jedi* poster under the washed-out yellow gleam of his lamp until he was disturbed by the sound of tapping coming from his bedroom door.

"Yeah?" he inquired, sitting up against his pillow.

The door opened and his mother came in. She was wearing her silky beige robe, and the lamplight gleamed against a tiny silver heart studded with red glass gemstones which hung from a chain around her neck. Though Corbin rarely saw this necklace, he knew that she always wore it under her shirt. His father had given it to her back when they first started dating, and she almost never took it off. Not even when she went to bed or took a shower, so far as Corbin knew.

"I just came in to say goodnight," she said as she approached the bed. "How do you like the new room?"

"It's nice," Corbin replied. "A lot bigger than my old room."

"Think you'll be able to sleep here all right?"

Corbin shrugged.

"Probably not so well at first," he answered honestly. "It's just … you know … new. And bigger. I'll get used to it."

She smiled at him sympathetically.

"You don't have to be embarrassed if there's anything else bothering you."

Corbin stared at her uncomprehendingly.

"If you're at all worried about what your uncle said about this place," she went on, "or about what your father told you about the Fallon boy, you know you can talk to me about it, right?"

Corbin nodded with sudden understanding, and then he shrugged indifferently.

"I know," he said. "Those stories don't bother me."

Emily seemed to be content with his answer. She smiled, nodded, and began to walk back toward the door.

"I'll see you in the morning."

There was so much that Corbin wanted to say. There were so many things that he wanted to know. At length, he called after her:

"What did Dad do to scare Uncle Kurt?"

Emily stopped, but she did not turn around. She stood with her back turned toward him for so long that Corbin began to wonder if she was going to walk out and pretend that she had not heard the question, but eventually, she did turn and started walking back toward the bed.

"What do you mean?" she asked.

"Uncle Kurt said, 'You had us scared for a while there,' " Corbin explained. "And Dad said that he had scared himself too."

Emily's posture changed, almost as if she was trying to lean away from the question. She stole a glance over her shoulder, and then she answered Corbin in a hushed voice:

"When things went bad with your grandfather and your dad and uncle had to move away, your father was very, very sad. He was sad and angry for a long time; long after your uncle had gotten over the whole thing and moved on. And when people are sad, sometimes they make mistakes. Sometimes, they…. Well, they can end up hurting themselves."

Corbin nodded thoughtfully.

"Like drinking and smoking," he concluded.

Emily cast another glance toward the door before nodding back at him.

"Yeah. Something like that."

A feeling of foreboding settled over Corbin as he recalled how, earlier that day, his father had almost bought a pack of cigarettes. His parents seemed to be happy now, but he had to wonder: Had his father's sadness and anger ever really gone away? Had he considered buying the cigarettes merely because it had become a habit? Corbin wondered if being sad and angry could become habits as well.

"Something you need to understand, Corbin," Emily went on, "is that your father has a lot of bad memories about this house. A lot of downright ugly ones. Your grandfather … was not a healthy person to be around."

Corbin did not dare to speak or even to move. He knew so little about what had happened between his father and his grandfather. At last, his mother seemed to be ready to talk about it, and he feared that if he did not keep absolutely still, the moment would be destroyed and he would never have a chance to hear the story again.

"Your father watched your grandfather lose his mind in this house," she finally said. "He started to become paranoid and delusional. He was convinced that there was something living in this house with them. Your father was only six years old when your grandfather uprooted their family, forcing them to leave in a single night to escape whatever he was seeing in his head.

"At first, your grandfather seemed to get a little better after that, but he never fully recovered. He started to become suspicious of his family, accusing them of taking his keys, or going through his things while he was at work, or conspiring against him behind his back. One night, your grandfather got the idea into his head that your father had taken something from him. He got rough with him, and … well, your father ended up in the hospital for three months."

Corbin stared at his mother, his eyes wide with wonder.

"When your father was discharged from the hospital," she continued, "he, your uncle, and your grandmother ran away to Catawba, North Carolina, to live with his uncle Michael and aunt Lisa."

"Where he met you," Corbin recalled.

"Yes," Emily replied, smiling at some distant memory. "You uncle Kurt introduced us. We've been together ever since."

"So, the ghost stories, then," Corbin ventured. "Is that where they all came from? From my grandfather?"

"I suppose that's where they all started," Emily said, "though the stories have gotten more colorful and a lot more plentiful as the years have passed. What you need to keep in mind, Corbin, is that, even though there's nothing here that can actually hurt us, coming back to this house was a very difficult thing for your father to do. It's been a lot harder for him than he's trying to let on, and we're going to have to be patient with him and try our hardest to make all of this work. This house may not be haunted—not in the traditional sense of the word—but it holds quite a few ghosts for him. Do you understand?"

Corbin nodded, and his mother smiled at him.

"I'm going to say goodnight now," she said.

"Goodnight, Mom."

His mother left, shutting the door behind herself. Corbin turned off his lamp and rolled over to face the wall, a thousand thoughts racing through his head.

My grandfather lost his mind here, Corbin thought. *And the Fallon boy. That's two. Two down; three to go.*

He squeezed his eyes tightly shut, hoping the pressure would push the thought out of his head.

There's nothing here that can actually hurt us....

Chapter Three
What Dreams May Come

That night, Corbin had a nightmare. He was standing alone in the midst of a charred and barren landscape. Far in the distance, looming over the horizon like an approaching storm, was a massive face made out of a churning cloud of smoke. Two blue suns pierced through the smoke like searchlights, their beams sweeping across the land, and the bottom portion of the cloud split open to form a monstrous smile.

Corbin instinctively knew that the face belonged to his grandfather. His grandfather knew that they had come to Devland, and his bright blue eyes were scouring the land in search of him. Though Corbin did not make the connection, the swollen and deformed visage that his subconscious mind had ascribed to his grandfather bore a striking resemblance to the clown poster in his father's old room.

The face in the sky let out a terrible, booming groan so loud that it threatened to split the earth. Its eyes swept left and right, back and forth, their beams of light coming so close to Corbin at times that he could scarcely believe that he had remained undetected. He wanted to crawl away and find cover—more than that, he wanted to give heed to his panic and run as far and as fast as he could—but fear kept him frozen in place.

"THE END HAS COME."

The mighty voice seemed to vibrate in Corbin's chest. His legs trembled and sweat was running down his face, yet he dared not move lest his grandfather should notice him. At last, he found the courage to take a single step backward. Gravel crunched beneath his bare foot, and suddenly, he was blinded as the glare of the searchlights fell directly upon him and a shrill voice seemed to scream directly into his right ear:

"*THERE YOU ARE!*"

Corbin came out of the dream shaking and damp with sweat. He sat up and began to gasp for breath, and for a moment, he did not recognize where he was. His breathing began to slow as memories of the day's events started to come back to him, and he slowly lay back down with a relieved sigh.

At first, he assumed that it was the dream that had awakened him, but then he heard a reedy, melodious voice coming from somewhere inside the house. He held his breath for a moment, uncertain as to whether the voice had been real or a lingering fragment of his dream, until he heard it again. Corbin struggled to sort through his half-woken thoughts, trying to remember if they might have left the television on. A feeling of dread began to swell within him as he came to the conclusion that somebody—an intruder, judging by the unfamiliar sound of their voice—was downstairs.

Corbin sat very still, listening. Over the sound of his own shallow breathing, he could hear the thin voice continuing to call out from somewhere below him. The voice had adopted a curious rhythm, as if the trespasser were singing a song, and Corbin began to recall how his father had said that it had become something of a rite of passage for young people to dare each other to spend the night in the haunted house on Butterwort Street.

Did the voice belong to a child, he wondered? Judging by its tone and cadence, Corbin began to speculate that it might be a little girl who had been coerced into sneaking into their house and was now singing a tune in an attempt to keep her spirits up.

Corbin draped his quilt over his shoulders and wrapped it across his chest with one arm. He silently set his feet down on the floor and stood up, determined to confront her and to make it known that the Wendell house was no longer open to ghost hunts, sleepovers, and shenanigans. He made his way to his bedroom door and tried to pull it open, but this proved to be much more difficult that he would have expected. Perhaps it was because of how tired he was, but it took him several good pulls to get the door to move at all. After he had managed to escape the bedroom, he proceeded to move down the shadowy hallway toward the stairs that led to the dining room.

When he reached his parents' room, he hesitated. For a moment, he thought about waking them, but something compelled him to go on without them. Even though he had not heard his name, he had a strange feeling that the voice was calling to him specifically. Was it one of the four bikers that he had seen that afternoon, he wondered? In any case, the voice was obviously coming from a child; it would be better, he decided, to let his parents sleep and deal with the intruder on his own.

As he made his way down the stairs, he observed that the trapdoor to the basement was open. He could not recall whether they had left it that way or not, but in any case, that was where the voice seemed to be coming from. The closer he came to the opening, the more aware he became of how distorted the voice sounded, as if it were echoing down a long corridor. He could not yet discern any specific words; all he could make out were the voice's gentle, almost hypnotic tone and its consistently rhythmic pacing.

He carefully descended the stairway into the basement, his footsteps as soft and silent as shadows, hoping to catch the prowler by surprise so that he might confront them before they ran off. When he reached the bottom of the steps, he could tell that the singing was coming from somewhere close by, but he was perplexed to find that there was not a soul to be seen.

His eyes began to comb the basement, sweeping every corner and peering into every shadow. He held his breath and listened, attempting to ascertain what direction the voice was coming from, until he finally determined that it was emanating from the narrow space between their washing machine and dryer. The far end of the gap was cloaked in darkness, but it scarcely seemed possible that anyone larger than an infant could have been concealed back there.

Be that as it may, the muffled vocalizations continued, and Corbin was certain that he had homed in on their source. He knelt down in front of the gap and stared into the inky blackness. He reached out with his hand, at that point expecting to find a radio or some similar device rather than a human being, and his fingers brushed across the floor and found nothing.

He turned himself sideways so that he might reach farther, and suddenly his arm dropped downward, and he realized that a part of the floor was missing. A surge of panic swept through him as his weight pitched forward and his whole arm plunged into frigid water. He felt as if a cable tied to his spine was being yanked backward, and he cried out as he was pulled back into his bed and woke up.

Corbin sat up abruptly. His whole body was tingling, and he felt more shaken and exhilarated than he could recall having ever felt in his life. Clearly, his walk down to the basement had been a dream, but somehow it felt like it had been more than that. It was like no dream he had ever had before, and he was convinced that it must have had some sort of meaning.

Was there something actually hidden in the back of that gap between their washing machine and dryer, he wondered? Had he caught a fleeting glimpse of it that afternoon and noted it on a subconscious level? If so, what might it be? A box full of stolen money? Hidden treasure? Bars of gold? His imagination running wild, he got to his feet and began to hurry across the room, almost running in his excitement to check the space between the washing machine and dryer. He reached the bottom of the stairway and stepped into the dining room, and then he stopped.

The trapdoor was open, just as it had been in his dream. For some reason, the mere sight of it turned his excitement to caution. He listened, half expecting to hear the voice from his dream once more, but he heard nothing. He realized that he was no longer anxious to venture down that last flight of steps. He dreaded to even look at it, lest he should find some unimaginable horror staring back at him. Finally, he walked over to the trapdoor and gently eased it shut, deliberately averting his eyes from the stairway as he did so.

    Corbin returned to his bed. He drifted restlessly in and out of sleep for the rest of the night, but he had no more dreams. Then, at five o'clock, he heard the harsh beeping of his parents' alarm clock in the next room, announcing the start of his father's first day at Doctor Wendell's Family Healthcare.

Chapter Four
Strange Faces

Corbin lay on his back for a while, listening. The sound of the alarm clock had ceased. He soon heard the sound of his parents' bedroom door opening, and then he heard their shuffling feet and low, murmuring voices. His bed creaked as he shifted his weight and set his feet down on the floor, and he remained seated like that for an even longer while. His neck was stiff, he could feel the pressure of his pulse slowly surging through his temples, and he felt more exhausted than he had in a long, long time.

It took all of his determination to force himself to stand up and begin changing into his day clothes. He was so tired that even the act of dressing proved difficult. He stomped around for a while with his pants partway up his left leg, his right foot catching on and tripping over the stubborn bundle that had entwined itself around his ankle. Eventually, he managed to finish the endeavor, touch-combed his hair by raking his fingers through it, and stepped out of his room to meet the day.

"Well, look who's here!"

His father was in the upstairs bathroom, buttoning up a white dress shirt. His voice conveyed a level of surprised amusement.

Corbin smiled back at him in spite of his weariness.

"I believe we had an appointment," he replied cordially.

"You appear to be right on time," James said. "Your mother's downstairs, getting ready to fix breakfast. If you hurry, you might be able to talk her into throwing a couple extra eggs in the pan."

Corbin nodded and shuffled toward the stairway. Upon entering the dining room, he saw that his mother was already at the stove, attending to a pan of eggs and another pan of sausages.

"Good morning," she said with a smile after she had noticed him. "I've got sausages coming up in a bit. I'll fix you some eggs after your father's are done. You want 'em over easy?"

"Yep," Corbin said with a nod. Then, recalling his manners in spite of his early-morning fuzziness, he added: "Thank you."

"Why don't you get yourself some juice and take a seat?"

Corbin nodded in reply. He fetched himself a small glass from the cupboard and opened the refrigerator. Inside, he saw orange, grape, and apple juice sitting on the top shelf. He filled his cup with the latter, and then he sat down at the table with his back toward the living room. A few moments later, his father came down the stairs, fully dressed and wearing a blue necktie.

"So," James addressed Corbin as he seated himself at the table with his face toward the kitchen, "you got any big plans for the day?"

Corbin shrugged, distractedly tracing a line across the table with the tip of his finger.

"Just hang around the house, mostly, I guess," he said, thinking that it might be more efficient to bring up the idea of riding his bike after his mother had joined them at the table. He asked his father:

"Do you know what Uncle Kurt's going to have you doing today?"

James shrugged.

"Based on what he told me last week," James explained, "it sounds like I'm mostly going to be watching and learning for now. He said he might let me put my signature on a prescription or escort patients to and from his office. Mostly he wants me to become familiar with the room, take note of where everything is, and pay close attention to how he *presents* himself to his patients."

He made this last remark with something close to a sneer.

"Evidently," James went on, "he has this very particular … I don't want to call it a 'mind game,' but that's kind of what it amounts to … that he plays with his patients. He said, 'The Wendell practice is not a big city hospital, nor is it the backwoods hut of your local witchdoctor.' He tries to walk a fine line between getting patients to laugh and feel like they're visiting family and making a complete ass of himself. Evidently, he's concerned that I might come across as too formal and too 'big city' for the locals to take a liking to."

Emily let out a barely perceptible groan as she approached the table.

"Your brother's such a megalomanic," she said, setting a mug of coffee and a plate with three over well eggs and four sausages in front of James. "You're a good man. You get on well with people. If you don't want to act like a clown and pretend to be everybody's second cousin, he should suck it up and start appreciating you for who you are."

She then hustled back toward the kitchen to retrieve Corbin's plate.

"*Thank* you," James said emphatically, seemingly more in regard to her statement than to the breakfast that she had set before him. "You should apply for work as his receptionist. It sounds like his office could use more of that kind of thinking."

Emily came back into the dining room, carrying Corbin's three sausages with a small, self-satisfied smile on her face. Now that his mother was in the room and his father had his breakfast in front of him, Corbin took advantage of the moment to blurt out:

"I was thinking, maybe I could get my bike out of the basement this morning. I'd kind of like to take it out for a spin; maybe see the rest of Devland."

His mother set his plate down slowly, a stern look on her face. James contemplatively chewed a mouthful of sausage. He seemed to notice Emily's expression, and he quickly forced the mouthful down his throat.

"Well, this ain't Morgantown," he reminded her. "I used to go on walks and ride my bike all over when I was his age."

"People are people wherever you go," Emily replied. "The only reason bad things seem to happen more often in big cities is because there are more people there for them to happen to. Besides, that was a long time ago. Just because your parents were okay with you riding your bike around town unsupervised back then doesn't mean that they'd be okay with it in this day and age."

"Oh, come on, Em," James scoffed. "This is Devland! I can't imagine that things here have changed all that much."

He gave Corbin a strange little smile and added: "Heck, I just saw a girl out riding her bike yesterday afternoon, so her parents must be okay with it!"

Corbin could feel his face beginning to redden, and he found an excuse to turn his gaze away from his father by becoming unduly engrossed in his sausages. He began to poke at them with his fork, rolling them back and forth across his plate, regarding their tone and texture with a forced level of interest.

Of course, he went there, Corbin moaned internally. *Always with some girl. "Do you like that girl, Corbin?... You should talk to this girl, Corbin."*

Corbin was at an age where the opposite sex held little more enticement for him than a sense of mild curiosity. He had barely been able to make friends with anyone at school, regardless of their gender, and his father's relentless prodding did little but embarrass him and make him even more hesitant to approach or be seen around girls.

Emily nodded thoughtfully, and then she told Corbin:

"I would want you to be back here by lunch time. Any later than that and I'll assume something has happened to you, and I'll be calling your father at work and we'll both be out looking for you. Is that fair enough?"

"I'll be here," Corbin assured her. "Thanks, Mom."

Emily headed back toward to the kitchen to prepare Corbin's over easy eggs, and Corbin gave his father a grateful look. James must have picked up on it, because he gave his son a grin and a quick wink before returning his attention to his breakfast.

After James had finished his eggs, sausages, and cup of coffee, he said his goodbyes and headed out the door. The white, hazy summer sky was just beginning to show the first traces of morning's light. Corbin figured that he still had about half an hour to wait before sunrise so decided to busy himself with checking out the small library of books in their sitting room.

The shelves were full of intimidatingly large hardcovers, many of which Corbin was vaguely familiar with: Charles Dickens's *David Copperfield;* Jane Austen's *Pride and Prejudice;* Herman Melville's *Moby Dick.* On the shelf second from the top, he spotted a copy of *Frankenstein; or, The Modern Prometheus* by Mary Shelley. This last discovery excited him. Though he was far more familiar with the Frankenstein movies than he was with the book, he had always found the story intriguing. He pulled the book from its place on the shelf and sat down on one of the sitting room's twin couches, eager to begin.

A mere few pages in, Corbin became dismayed. He found that he almost needed a thesaurus to make sense of some of the words, and the grammar in some of the sentences was so archaic that it took an unpleasant amount of effort for him to grasp their meaning. He knew that the story had been written a long time ago—in the late seventeen hundreds or early eighteen hundreds, if he remembered correctly—and he suspected that the book must have presented a much more casual reading experience for people who had lived back then.

It occurred to him that perhaps an adult would have an easier time getting through the *Frankenstein* book. The thought flickered across his mind just long enough to make him furrow his brow in annoyance. He was old enough, he reminded himself, to read anything that an adult could make sense of. He did not actually need a thesaurus to understand the more archaic words; he could deduce their basic meanings by the context that they were presented in, and he became all the more determined to not only read the book, but to enjoy it.

He became so invested in this endeavor that, before he knew it, over an hour had passed. He suddenly realized that it was already nearly a quarter after seven and that the sun was shining hotly in the eastern sky. He hastened to put the book back on the shelf where he had found it and walked into the dining room.

"I'm headed out," Corbin told his mother. She looked up from the box that she was unpacking on the dining room table and nodded at him acceptingly.

"Lunch is at eleven," she told him.

"I'll be here," he promised, and he walked past her toward the trapdoor over the basement.

The terrors of the previous night having been chased away by the light of day, Corbin ventured down the steps without hesitation or fear. He still half expected to find something of value, or at least of interest, in the space between the washing machine and dryer, but the sun was shining through the window, revealing nothing but a bare concrete floor.

Upon observing this, Corbin began to feel foolish. Of course, there was nothing there. What had he been thinking? Had he really believed that he had received some sort of psychic revelation or that the voice in his dream had been that of a ghost guiding him toward some long-lost treasure? Perhaps, he reasoned, he had merely been so caught up in the rush of the moment that he had not given the matter any amount of logical thought at all.

He grasped the handlebars of his bike and swung his leg over the top tube, alighting gently upon the seat. The years since he had last ridden seemed to wash away as he almost instinctively recalled the bike's weight and balance, raised the kickstand, and pedaled effortlessly toward the door on his left.

    Corbin pushed the bike up the concrete steps into their backyard and out into the street, and then he began to do laps and figure eights in front of the house. He felt a surge of exhilaration as he rode faster and faster, allowing the moist breeze to cool the sweat that was beginning to form on his brow, yet he did not stray far. Something held him back from exploring the neighborhood as he had initially planned. Maybe it was a need to play it cautious until he felt that he had become fully reacquainted with the bike. Or perhaps it was because it had been there that he had seen the other bikers and he was hoping that they would pass by that way again. If it was the latter reason that kept him close to home, his patience was soon to be rewarded, for after less than an hour's time, he caught sight of two figures approaching from the west.

    He recognized the heavy-set boy with the buzzed hair and the white bike, and behind him was the girl with the golden hair and the black Cannondale. Corbin's heart began to race, and he turned his back on them to complete another figure-eight formation. He glided back past the house and turned toward them again hopefully.

    Neither of the bikers had approached him. The boy was observing Corbin with both of his feet on the ground and his arms crossed, muttering something that Corbin had no hope of making out from that distance. The girl was more animated, steadying her bike with one leg and nodding in Corbin's direction as if urging her companion onward. The boy with the buzzed hair's dark eyes glistened in the sunlight like wet, black stones as he regarded Corbin, shook his head in what might have been disagreement with whatever the girl had said, and began to slowly pedal his Trek Madone forward.

    Corbin and the other boy passed each other on opposite sides of the street. There was a brief, awkward interlude where the two of them continued to perform circles and loops in front of the house, neither one of them stopping or bothering to address the other's presence. For Corbin, this was nothing less than torture. He had wanted nothing more than to find these bikers. As it turned out, they had found him, and now that they had, he realized that he had no idea what he should do next.

Should I pull over and try to say hello? he agonized over his options. *Should I take his advance as an invitation and just ride off with him toward the west? Should I call out to him and ask him his name? Or just follow his lead and keep circling? What if I take too long to make up my mind and they both get tired of this and just ride off without me?*

The lanky boy with the red Roubaix appeared next to the girl, and the boy on the white bike seemed to take this as his cue to bring himself to a stop in front of Corbin.

"Is your father James Wendell?"

The boy's voice was deep and cold. Corbin pulled up in front of him and set a foot on the ground to steady himself, his stomach churning so strongly that he feared he might vomit. He nodded in affirmation and then asked:

"How do you know my dad?"

The boy on the white bike shrugged.

"It's a small town," he said. "Everybody's been talking about how Doctor Wendell's brother came back to Devland. Doctor Wendell has owned this house for years, and he's never been able to get anybody else to rent it from him, so it wasn't that hard to guess. Dominic Moretti. Don, if you like."

"Corbin." Sweat was beginning to sting his eyes now that he had been denied the breeze that had come from movement.

"It's a pleasure to meet you, Corbin," Dominic said, and he put on a polite smile. "Follow me, and I'll introduce you to the others."

Corbin gave what he hoped would pass as a casual nod, though his heart was fairly well leaping with excitement. He followed Dominic down Butterwort Street to where the other boy and the blonde girl sat waiting for them.

"This is Corbin Wendell," Dominic called as he pulled up in front of them.

"Thomas Link," the boy on the red bike introduced himself with a hearty grin.

"Angela," the girl said. Her tone was friendly, though Corbin noticed that she seemed to be struggling to maintain eye contact.

"We were about to head out to Clair's," Dominic explained. "We're gonna pick up some creamsicle bars and cokes and go hang out at the waterfall."

"Well, it's not exactly a waterfall," Thomas elaborated.

"It's kind of what we do over the summer," Dominic told Corbin, seemingly displeased with Thomas's interjection. "You'll see it when we get there, if you're of a mind to come with us."

Corbin was elated at their invitation, but he was also terrified. He had always found it difficult to make new friends, much less keep them, and he was consumed with fear that he might say something wrong. Furthermore, he had promised his mother that he would be back by eleven. He knew that Clair's General Store and Deli was at the edge of town, and he had no idea how far it was from there to the waterfall that was not exactly a waterfall. He debated in his mind whether he should accept their invitation or simply retreat to the safety of his own house.

"You really should come," the girl named Angela prodded him. Her bright blue eyes finally locked with his, and she smiled warmly. "We've been anxious to get to know you. We were sort of hoping we might get to add a new rider to our little group."

Corbin smiled back at her, looked down at his feet uncomfortably, and returned his gaze to Dominic.

"I'll go as far as Clair's," he finally consented. "I don't know if I can make it as far as the waterfall, though. I promised my mother that I'd be back early."

"*Lame*," Thomas moaned with a sardonic grin, and Corbin felt a small part of himself die.

"However far you'd care to go," Angela said, casting a reproachful glance at Thomas, "we'd be glad to have the extra company."

"We'll be meeting up with Raven Moore along the way," Dominic said. "She lives over on Paisley Street. It's just a little bit out of our way."

Without another word, he began to speed off to the west, and the others were quick to follow suit.

"Try to keep up!" Thomas called out. Corbin hesitated one last moment, and then he began to pedal his bike in fierce pursuit.

They followed Butterwort Street to where it curved to the left and intersected with Margo Street, at which point Dominic made a right onto the sidewalk. Already worried about how long the trip was going to take, Corbin was dismayed by the realization that they were moving still farther away from Clair's. His worries were put to rest less than a minute later, however, when they came to a stop at a crosswalk and Corbin saw a sign for Paisley Street directly across from them.

Dominic waited for a slowing in the traffic, and then he sped across Margo Street. Thomas was the next to venture across, prompting the driver of a Volkswagen to tap on his brakes and let out an indignant blast of his horn. A few seconds later, Angela and Corbin found an opening and were able to follow them.

They rode past several townhouses before pulling over on the left side of the street. The house that they had stopped at was a rundown, two-story structure adorned with overgrown shrubs and a partially collapsed wooden deck that was listing dangerously to the left. A familiar silver Lynskey bike was sitting on the deck, propped up against the railing.

The blinds across one of the windows rustled momentarily, and then the black-haired girl Corbin had seen the day before came shuffling out of the house. Her hands were buried in the pockets of a well-worn black jacket, the hood of which was pulled over her head. She remained standing on the deck for a few seconds, regarding the four of them, and then she grasped the handlebars of her bike and came forward to meet them.

"This is Corbin Wendell!" Dominic introduced Corbin with a seemingly forced air of merriment. "Corbin, this is Raven. She completes our little band. We hang out together almost every day over the summer. Mostly at the waterfall, but there's other things to do in Devland too."

"Yeah," Raven grunted, her eyes fixed upon the pavement. "The *four* of us have all kinds of fun together."

Corbin noticed the emphasis she placed on the word "four," and he interpreted it as a hint that she did not approve of the others having invited a fifth member to their ranks. Angela seemed to have picked up on the inference as well, and she shot Raven a poisonous glare. Raven's dark eyes squinted back at her, and Angela immediately dropped her gaze.

"Corbin's riding with us far as Clair's," Dominic said, seemingly unaware of, or possibly ignoring, the exchange which had just taken place. "We're hoping that he might stick with us as far as the waterfall, but he can't stay out too late, apparently."

"Oedipus complex," Thomas explained without a trace of hostility.

"Just as well," Raven said. Though her expression bore an unmistakable flicker of resentment, her voice was surprisingly docile. "You probably wouldn't like it. It's just a bit of runoff from a creek that splashes when it hits the rocks. Nothing spectacular."

"I believe what really makes the waterfall special," Thomas said, looking at Angela as if expecting to elicit a response from her, "is the people that you get to experience it with. I think the lowliest mudpuddle can be a thing of beauty, if one gets to see it with people that they care about. Wouldn't you say?"

"What are you tryin' to be?" Dominic grunted. "A goddamn poet?"

Thomas opened his mouth as if to reply, but Dominic cut him off.

"Whatever. I don't care. We've got our mission and we're all on board with it, yeah? Last one to Clair's is buying!"

With that, Dominic abruptly wheeled his bike around and sped off toward Margo Street, and the others scrambled to catch up with him.

"He's lying," Thomas shouted at Corbin.

Corbin glanced over at Thomas in confusion.

"About the loser buying lunch," Thomas elaborated, his voice elevated to compete with the wind in their ears. "He's not being serious. It's just something that he likes to say."

They turned right onto the sidewalk on the south side of Margo Street. From there on, Dominic set them on a pace that Corbin found almost frantic. His legs began to burn and the hot, humid air that blew against his face was no longer enough to keep the sweat from matting his hair and soaking through his shirt, but he refused to complain or allow himself to fall behind. By the time they had come within sight of Clair's, Corbin's face was burning and he was gasping for breath, and he was almost grateful that he had previously made an excuse about not being able to ride the rest of the way with them.

Dominic was the first to ride into the parking lot. He circled back behind the others as they came in, almost as if he felt some moral obligation to make sure the rest of the group had alighted before doing so himself. Angela and Thomas pulled up along a curb close to the street. Corbin rode past them and brought his bike to a stop next to Raven. She seemed to notice his rapid breathing, and she raised a questioning eyebrow.

"You gonna live?" she asked.

Corbin kept his eyes fixed straight ahead, but he forced a smile onto his face and replied coolly:

"Yeah, I'm not dyin' today. You'll have to try harder than that."

Suddenly, Dominic's bike pulled in between them, so close to him that Corbin instinctively shifted his weight and almost tipped his bike onto its side. The burly boy eyed Corbin almost resentfully for a moment, and then his expression changed to a satisfied grin.

"You kept up just fine," he told Corbin as he dropped his kickstand and dismounted. "Might keep you around yet."

The air inside Clair's was air-conditioned and refreshing. Corbin's four companions took their time at the chilled bins, though the lack of interest with which they regarded their varied contents led Corbin to believe that they had made up their minds about what they were getting before they got there: all four of them picked out orange creamsicle bars, and Dominic, Thomas, Angela, and Raven chose bottles of Coca-Cola, Fanta Orange Soda, Sprite, and A&W Root Beer, respectively. Corbin decided to forgo the ice cream bars and settled for a cold Doctor Pepper.

"So," Corbin began with a hint of shame in his voice as they approached the checkout counter. For some reason he had been grasped by the feeling that all of the progress that he had made that day was standing upon the edge of a precipice, and he chose his words with exquisite care. "Before I left this morning, I promised my mother that I wouldn't stay out too late. I've had a great time, and I really would like to see the waterfall—"

"No worries, brother," Dominic cut him off with an impatient wave of his hand. "It was good riding with you. I hope we didn't scare you off with the pace we set this morning. We don't always ride that hard. Not in this kind of heat anyway."

"No, that's not it!" Corbin assured him, his face flushing at the implication. "I just really need to get back."

"Maybe you'll ride with us again tomorrow?" Angela ventured, her voice sounding hopeful.

Corbin smiled uncomfortably, and he started to scrape at the label on his bottle of Doctor Pepper with his thumbnail.

"Yeah, we'll see!"

"Next time, you should come with us to the waterfall," Thomas urged him. "Tell your mom you'll be going with friends. Shit, I'll even give you my parents' phone number, if that makes it easier for you. Just so she has some idea of who you're gonna be with, you know?"

Corbin was touched by their evident determination to add him to their numbers, and he fixed all of his attention on his peeling of the Doctor Pepper label in an effort to conceal his rapidly welling excitement.

"Maybe," he agreed. Then he quickly added, "I appreciate it."

"It's a date, then!" Dominic said. "We'll swing by your place to collect you at around seven."

After they had all paid for their drinks and snacks, the four bikers rode off to the east, leaving Corbin behind. He gulped at his Doctor Pepper, anxious to finish it and free up his hands for the ride home. His imagination was running rampant and he realized that his legs were trembling as he mounted his bike, and throughout the entire ride home, he fantasized about how much better the next day, the coming school year, and life in general had the potential to be.

During lunch that morning, as he and his mother ate peanut butter and jelly sandwiches, Corbin talked about his ride to Clair's. She seemed quite pleased to hear that he had made new friends, and he found that she was surprisingly receptive to the idea of his staying out a bit longer the next day.

"You should go with them," she encouraged. "This waterfall seems to mean a lot to them. If they want to show it to you, it's only polite that you check it out once and let them know what you think of it."

Corbin was aware that her encouragement had little to do with his checking out the waterfall or with being polite. He knew that she was happy that he was finally starting to fit in somewhere, and she clearly did not want to let the opportunity go to waste.

"Fine," he replied with a shrug that masked his nearly overwhelming eagerness. "They wanted to meet up at seven tomorrow."

"That'd be fine," she said with a smile. "What time did you want me to wake you up? Six thirty? Does that give you enough time to get ready?"

"I was gonna get up at five," Corbin explained. Though he had gotten up at five that morning with the ulterior motive of getting an early start at riding his bike, he had enjoyed having breakfast with his father.

His mother looked pleased and said:

"I'm sure your father would like that."

"If I hear your alarm go off?"

"I'll be sure to stomp my feet when I go downstairs," she said in a conspiratorial whisper.

That afternoon, Corbin busied himself with attempting to read *Frankenstein* until his head started to hurt, at which point he turned on the television on the chance that his father had called the cable company from work. There were still no channels available, so he elected to turn on the DVD player and rewatch *Silent Hill*.

James arrived home shortly before five thirty, by which time Emily had nearly finished preparing a dinner of seasoned chicken breasts, canned corn, and macaroni and cheese. After

James had washed up, the three of them sat down in the dining room together.

"How did it go at the salt mines?" Emily asked.

"Easy-peasy!" James waved his hand dismissively and grinned at her. "My brother's still waiting for me to prove something or other to him, I guess. Mostly I just listened to what he had to say, fetched things for him, and made polite small talk with the patients. He has a vacant room in the back, though. He said that it's going to be mine and that I'll be seeing my own patients there soon, after he's satisfied that I'm ready."

James's face beamed with pride after he had announced this last bit of news.

"Corbin made some new friends today," Emily told him.

"Oh, did he, now?" James said with what struck Corbin as little more than a veneer of interest. "Well, that's great, Corbin! Was it the two kids that were out riding bikes yesterday?"

Corbin realized that his father had been quite proud of his announcement that Uncle Kurt was preparing to give him his own private office soon, and he had obviously been wounded by the manner in which his mother had so quickly changed the subject.

"Yep," Corbin answered shortly, determined to return the conversation to his father's practice as quickly as possible. "What about you, Dad? You making friends at work?"

James exhaled deeply and looked down at his plate as if struggling with an unpleasant memory, and then he let out a disparaging laugh and shook his head.

"Uncle Kurt really needs to fire Josh," he finally said.

"Josh?" Emily inquired.

"Yeah. Josh. You remember, Em. I talked about him yesterday. Kurt's gopher boy?"

"I remember you said something about him."

"Well, he's just a lawsuit waiting to happen," James said. "That kid has no respect for anyone. About all he did all day was mock the patients behind their backs and make insensitive jokes about their ailments. At one point, he escorted this one particularly large man down the hall, and the whole time Josh was behind him he was imitating the guy's walk, doing some stupid 'fat-man waddle.' "

"Sounds like a real winner of a human being," Emily replied sourly.

"Yeah," James grunted. "But it seems like Kurt is fine with it! Josh is good at not getting caught. You know, he puts on his polite little smile when the patients are looking at him, but as soon as their backs are turned, he starts acting like a complete dick. But Uncle Kurt doesn't seem to care, so what are you gonna do about it?

"And then there's Missus Sherman," James went on. "A wretched old thing. She's set in her ways and can't stand anything new. And when I say 'anything new,' I'm referring to myself. But they tell me that she just takes a while to adjust to people and that she'll take to me eventually, so there's that to look forward to, I guess. About the only real silver lining to this cloud is Doctor Goodman."

"You two get along all right, then?" Emily asked.

"Swimmingly!" James said. "If I survive this at all, it'll be thanks to Doctor Goodman."

"I'm glad to hear that Corbin's not the only one that made a new friend today," Emily said. "We should invite him to dinner some evening!"

James looked at Emily in apparent bewilderment.

"Doctor Goodman, you mean?"

"Sure! Do you think he'd be up for it?"

James dropped his eyes to his plate and began to use his fork to rearrange his kernels of corn.

"I don't know," he said with a half-hearted shrug. "I mean, I could ask, but … I guess I'm not sure we're close enough for all that yet. You know?"

Corbin considered the way his father had wilted at the suggestion of asking Doctor Goodman to dinner. It occurred to him that his father might have harbored more admiration for Goodman than Goodman felt toward him. He hoped that his father would go on to earn the respect of all of new coworkers, even Josh and Missus Sherman. At least, for the most part, his parents still seemed happy with their new lives in Devland, and that was what really mattered.

Shortly after eight thirty, the Wendell family started to work their way through the nightly routine of brushing teeth and changing into sleepwear. Corbin made it into bed just before nine o'clock, and it did not take him long to fall into a deep sleep. Then, at about midnight, he found himself sitting upright and gasping for breath, having been torn from the depths of his slumber by the sound of a familiar, haunting melody.

Chapter Five
Stranger Places

Corbin sleepily rubbed at his eyes.

Is this a dream?

He lowered his hands from his face and stared down at his palms. He observed their familiar creases and the seemingly genuine manner in which his fingers folded as he curled his hands into fists. His hands looked real enough, but given his experience on the previous night, he was fairly certain that he was dreaming.

He crossed the room and proceeded to pull his bedroom door open, finding the endeavor no less difficult than it had been on the previous night. Even though he was aware that he was dreaming, he felt compelled to investigate the voice. It was as if he had been dropped in the middle of a stage play, and all that he could remember about his role was that he was supposed to move toward the source of the singing and meet ... someone? *Who?* It seemed that he had forgotten, but that did not change the nature of his part in the play, so he continued to move obediently forward.

When he reached the door to his parents' room, he hesitated once more. He wondered, if he were to open the door, would he see his parents in his dream? Might they be dreaming as well? If they were, would they be able to see him, and could he convince them to come down to the basement with him? He was so intrigued by these questions that he ventured to try the doorknob, but he found that he was unable to grasp it. His fingers seemed to glide just over the knob's surface, almost as if his hand and the knob shared a common magnetic polarity, and he was forced to abandon the effort and continue down to the basement on his own.

He knelt in front of the space between the washing machine and dryer. He turned sideways and slid his torso into the narrow gap, reaching with his arm until his hand dipped into the pool of cold water once more. Then, after taking a brief moment to remind himself that he was dreaming and that no harm could come to him, he threw caution to the wind and pitched his body forward into the pool's frigid depths.

Corbin found himself floating in icy water. The shock of the water washing over him and filling his nostrils almost caused him to panic, but then, far above him, he saw a glimmer of light. He swam toward it until his head had broken the surface of the pool and he gasped for breath, shivering with cold.

Before him lay a long, wet tunnel lit by an array of wooden torches. The torches seemed to be sunken into the tunnel's stone walls, almost as if they had been there for centuries and the rock had formed around them. Corbin observed that most of the torches had gone out, but a few of them were still burning, casting a wavering orange glow upon the tunnel's crooked walls and causing the shadows to dance around him. From somewhere further down the tunnel, he could hear the clear and mesmerizing sound of a girl singing.

He climbed out over the rocky ledge that encircled the pool and set his feet down on the rough, downward-slanting floor of the tunnel. As he slowly shuffled forward, his body still shivering and his teeth starting to chatter, he took note of how the torches were set on either side of the tunnel at unequal and seemingly random intervals. The first two that he passed had gone out, but the next one on his left was still burning. Corbin reached out his hand to take it, but he was repelled by an airy hissing sound. He drew his hand back in alarm, and then his eyes located the source of the sound: an eight-inch-long, black, oily-looking grasshopper that was sitting on an overhanging rock formation.

The insect took a wary step backward as Corbin extended his arm once more and took hold of the torch. After several tugs, the torch came free of the wall in a small avalanche of flakey, shale-like chips of stone. With this newly acquired light source held high, Corbin resumed his journey down the tunnel, drawing ever closer to the enticing melody which had disturbed his slumber.

    Corbin's heart was beating fast, and he was beginning to feel the same excitement that he had felt on the previous night, as if he was on the verge of discovering something of incredible importance. As he went on, his feet feeling numb and clumsy against the damp stone and his soaked pajamas clinging uncomfortably to his body, he began to make out some of the words of the song:

> *What it is, I do not know,*
> *But I had so very far to go.*
> *So many trials to overcome,*
> *So very much to see.*
> *Ignored her call*
> *To find a box.*
> *I lost it all,*
> *And found it locked.*
> *Should I regret all that I've done*
> *To bring it back to me?*

    These words meant nothing to Corbin, but they heightened his excitement and fortified his resolve to find the phantom singer. Eventually, he saw an opening at the end of the tunnel. There, squatting with its back toward him, was a strange creature. By its size and proportions, it looked rather like a child wearing a stiff, glossy cape, but its hair was thin and white and its wrinkled skin was sagging off of its body and in a manner that suggested old age and emaciation. As Corbin drew closer, he realized that what he had initially mistaken for a rigid cape was in fact a set of iridescent, wasp-like wings growing out from between the creature's shoulders.

The creature stopped singing. Its head came up with a start and it turned around to face Corbin. The creature was wearing a loincloth and had a green shawl thrown over its shoulders, the middle of which hung down behind the creature as far as its buttocks and the ends of which partially covered its sagging, mottled breasts. Its face looked more ancient than any living thing Corbin had ever seen, and he saw that it was cradling a small wooden box in its arms. The creature bared its dog-like teeth at him, rustled its wings, clutched the box tightly to its bosom, and began to flee into the darkness that lay beyond the mouth of the tunnel.

"Wait!" Corbin cried and began to pursue the creature. The tunnel opened up into a spacious cavern with a ceiling that was over twenty feet high and walls that spread outward until they became lost in shadows that might have been endless. The cavern was full of oak trees that had become bent and twisted, growing sideways and coiling around each other under the low ceiling in such a manner that it was difficult to discern between their gnarly branches and their bulging roots. There were black metal braziers hanging from the ceiling by chains, and there were a few braziers set into the crooks of branches as well. Several of the braziers contained red, smoldering embers, but most of them appeared to have gone cold.

Corbin stumbled through the subterranean forest, ducking under branches and tripping over roots with nothing to aid him but the braziers and the flickering light of his windswept torch. Cracked, rotten acorns had formed a thick blanket upon the floor, and they crunched and oozed beneath the soles of his feet as he laboriously made his way forward. As he proceeded, the forest became thicker and the trees became larger and more deformed, and his eagerness to catch up to the creature began to wane and to be replaced by a nagging feeling of unease.

After a few minutes of aimless wandering, Corbin started to hear whispers and rustling sounds coming from the darkness around him. He began to turn about slowly, waving the torch from side to side. Every time he turned, he would catch glimpses of an ever-increasing number of creatures peering down at him, roosting among the oak trees' broken branches or hugging their trunks. Ancient, feminine forms with slender white fingers and purplish, semi-translucent wings bared their teeth, hissed, and moved to conceal themselves whenever his eyes fell upon them.

Corbin's unease began to turn to panic as he realized that he was surrounded by these creatures. He was about to make a run for the pool through which he had come when an agile form no taller than a ten-year-old boy leaped out of a tree and landed directly in front of him. The creature wore black pants, a red shirt, a dark purple vest and black fingerless leather gloves, all of which were tattered and heavily soiled. Its eyes were emerald green and livid, and the skin on its deformed and elongated face was taut and stubbly. It had long, wolfish ears, and there were long and greasy tendrils of curly black hair dangling from beneath the leather beanie on its head.

The creature smiled maliciously.

"You don't belong here," it said in a surprisingly resonant voice. It lunged forward and shoved both of its hands into Corbin's chest, knocking the torch out of his hand and sending him reeling off balance.

The creature's sudden appearance and the shove were enough to shock Corbin into wakefulness. Once more, he felt as if a tether attached to his spine were being yanked backward, and suddenly he was in his bed again, tingling as if a current had passed through his body.

He sat upright, his heart racing. He felt nauseated, and it seemed as if his mouth was producing more saliva than he could bring himself to swallow. He sat for close to a minute with his legs folded and his arms cradling his stomach, rocking back and forth and allowing drool to fall into his lap, gasping for breath and trying not to vomit. After the attack had begun to subside, he forced his breathing back into a slow, steady rhythm, calming his mind by fixing his thoughts on a particular fold in his green and blue quilt.

Eventually, he was able to lie back down. He tossed and turned for nearly an hour, after which he became relaxed to the point that he might have gone back to sleep if a curious thing had not caught his attention: his bedroom door was hanging halfway open, and he could not for the life of him remember if he had left it that way when he had gone to bed.

Chapter Six
Hidden Things

Eventually, Corbin did manage to go back to sleep, and by the time his parents' alarm went off at five, he found himself feeling much better than he had on the previous morning. Those last few hours of undisturbed sleep had done wonders for him, and the fear that his nightmare had instilled in him had been replaced by the thrill of having a story to tell.

Initially, his parents listened to the tale of his nocturnal wanderings with evident amusement, but their expressions betrayed increasing levels of bafflement as the story went on. After he had finished, an uncomfortable silence prevailed over the dining room. At last, James dropped his eyes to his plate, shrugged nonchalantly, and started cutting one of his sausages.

"I would not dwell on these dreams if I were you, Corbin," he advised. "Having bad dreams can become a cycle. The more you allow yourself to become fascinated by them, the more likely you are to keep having them."

Emily stood rooted to the spot by the kitchen door, holding Corbin's eggs captive and showing no sign of releasing them. Finally, she ventured:

"Corbin, do you…. Do you have any memories of your grandfather?"

Corbin stared back at his mother in wonderment, a feeling of imminent realization beginning to scratch at the back of his mind.

"Why?" he asked. "Did my grandfather dream about the creatures under the basement too? Did he see them before he—"

Corbin found himself unable to finish the sentence aloud.
Before he lost his mind?
"No!"

The word shot out of James's mouth, forceful and harsh, and Corbin was not sure whether it was an answer to his question or a warning to his mother to keep silent.

"Your grandfather had dreams," James admitted reluctantly. He spoke in a kinder tone now, but his eyes remained stern. "Not quite like what you're describing, though. Don't let these dreams scare you, Son. Having dreams—even vivid ones, that seem like the realest thing in the world—is normal enough. Especially in strange, new places. Your grandfather went…. Well…. I believe he became the way he is, in part, because he let himself get to the point where he could no longer tell the difference between dreams and reality. You've got a lot going for you here, Corbin. You just made new friends! You're about to start at a new school! That's what's real. That's what matters. These are the things that your mind should be dwelling on. And, if you do have any more of these dreams, I would suggest that you don't go chasing after them. They're not real. There's nothing there for you to find. Do you understand?"

"Yes, sir," Corbin muttered feebly. He did, in truth, understand what his father was telling him, but he was once again needled by the suspicion that his parents were keeping something from him. Some detail of his dream had set them on edge; something had reminded them of his grandfather. His mother finally came forward with his eggs, and Corbin thanked her and began to solemnly pick at his breakfast.

James left for work that morning at about forty past five. Corbin still had nearly an hour and half until his friends were due to show up, so he retreated to the sitting room to seek distraction via their library of books. He decided to take a break from *Frankenstein*. The book had not defeated him—he would never allow that—but he reminded himself that there were other books in the world and that there was no shame in switching things up now and then.

Searching through the shelves, Corbin's eye landed upon a book that had previously escaped his notice: *Through the Looking-Glass, and What Alice Found There* by Lewis Carroll. He had heard of it and knew that, if memory served, it was regarded as a classic work of some importance, so he took it with him to the couch and settled in to read it.

The book started off with an introduction in the form of a poem that talked about the end of summer. In it, the author referred to himself as an aged child who worried about the approach of bedtime, and Corbin was certain that the whole thing was a metaphor representing the passing of youth and the inevitability of death. Corbin supposed that the poem was a fitting start for the book, because the story that followed was rather disturbing.

The book introduced its readers to a troubled little girl with a perverse fascination with punishing others and being punished. It was quickly established that this girl, Alice by name, was in the habit of imagining herself as multiple persons, had once terrified a woman by screaming that she was of a mind to gnaw upon her, and was in the habit of carrying on conversations with her cats. In truth, however, the more Corbin read, the less certain he became that the white and black kittens were real and the more he began to suspect that they were allegories of good and evil.

Corbin's heart broke when he read Alice's confession that she would rather starve for fifty days than be allowed to eat her fill, and he found it disturbing that she expressed her anger toward the black kitten by kissing it. Corbin could barely comprehend how tormented Alice must have been to have developed such self-destructive tendencies, and he could only imagine what a complicated family life she must have had if she interpreted a display of affection as a form of punishment. Soon, however, the story transformed into a bizarre fantasy about life on the other side of a mirror. The symbolism of this abrupt shift in literary style, if any, was lost on Corbin, and he found himself longing for the relative simplicity of Mary Shelley's writing.

The book's disjointed plot and warped sense of logic were beginning to make Corbin's head spin by the time seven o'clock arrived, at which point he ceased from his labors and went to the window facing Butterwort Street. He peeled back the venetian blinds and saw that Thomas and Angela were circling back and forth in front of his driveway. Thomas was popping wheelies, and both of them were laughing merrily.

Corbin quickly headed toward the trapdoor in the dining room, allowing the blinds to fall back against the window with a loud clatter.

"I'm headed out!" he shouted toward the stairs leading upstairs. He did not hear a reply. Corbin did not dare leave the house without his mother's permission, so he ventured upstairs to seek her out. He found her in his parents' room, sitting cross-legged on the bed, the iPad in her lap casting an icy blue glow onto her face.

"I'm headed out," Corbin repeated.

Emily momentarily looked up from the screen and gave him a smile.

"Have fun," she said. "Be safe out there."

"I will," Corbin replied, and then he made his way down to the basement. He grabbed his bike by the handlebars and pushed it up the back steps, not bothering to cast so much as a backward glance toward the narrow space between their washing machine and dryer.

"*Wendell!*" Thomas cried exultantly. Corbin smiled and waved awkwardly, squinting against the glare of the sun and the heat of the day. He mounted his bike and rode out into the street. Thomas swooped toward him with his hand held out, seemingly revving up to give him a forceful high-five. Corbin winced and braced his arm for the impact, but at the last moment, Thomas withdrew his arm and swerved so close that Corbin nearly lost control of his bike in his effort to avoid being knocked over.

Corbin could feel his face beginning to burn in a manner that had nothing to do with the Georgia heat. He noticed that Angela was laughing at his frustration, and he decided that it would be best to dismiss the incident as well-meaning horseplay. He let out a laugh as well and started to ride, moving back and forth in circles and figure eights in front of the house, though he kept a wary distance from Thomas. A few minutes later, he saw Dominic approaching from the west, followed by Raven.

"Ready and waiting!" Dominic observed with a smile. "So, what'll it be? Are you fixing to bail on us at Clair's, or are you gonna come and hang out at the waterfall?"

"I was thinking," Corbin said, bringing his bike to a stop in front of Dominic and setting his leg down for balance, "that, this time, I'd go all the way."

"That's the spirit!" Dominic said and gave Corbin an approving thumbs-up. Angela pulled up beside him, smiling brightly.

"You got a backpack?" Raven called to him from over Dominic's shoulder. "Or were we just going to skip Clair's this time?"

"Nah, we've got this," Dominic muttered without looking at her.

"I've got room in my pack," Thomas suggested, smiling broadly as he brought his bike to a stop between Corbin and Angela. "Whatever you want to get, buddy. Just throw it up on my back, and I will carry it for you. It's what friends are for, right?"

Once more, he cast a look at Angela that seemed to be begging for some sign of approval. Her smile faltered a little, and she busied herself by visually inspecting the chain on her bike.

"That's very touching, Thomas," Dominic said gruffly. "Okay, guys! Mount up! Last one there…."

The tail end of the sentence was lost in the wind as he sped away.

"… Is buying," Thomas finished, giving Corbin a weary grin as he started pedaling after Dominic and Raven. Angela hung back for a second, regarding Corbin with what he interpreted as a level of amusement, and then took off abruptly.

Angela stayed ahead of Corbin for the entire ride, but not by much. From time to time, she would look over her shoulder and adjust her rate, almost as if she were trying to keep Corbin and herself close together but at a distance from the others. Corbin also noticed a correlation between her backward glances and how she handled her bike: every look in his direction was almost unfailingly followed by her either rising out of her seat and standing at full height upon the pedals, or by her swerving her bike back and forth in a nearly suicidal fashion, or at the very least, by a change in her general posture. She seemed to be making an effort to hold his attention, and she succeeded to the point that, if she had not turned into the parking lot at Clair's, he would have ridden right past it without noticing.

Corbin pulled up beside her. His eyes were stinging with sweat, and both of them were breathing heavily. Now that he was sitting still, the humidity coupled with the heat rising off of his own body was nearly overwhelming, but he smiled at Angela nonetheless.

"That was…."

Corbin almost said "exhausting," but given the show that she seemed to have put on for him, he thought she might take the remark as an insult.

"… *awesome*."

He allowed the word to fall out of his mouth with all of the grace of a torn paper bag dumping groceries onto the pavement, and he immediately felt like a fool. In spite of this, Angela smiled back at him, and Corbin let out a relieved chuckle.

"What's funny?" she asked.

Corbin shrugged uncomfortably.

"I dunno."

Dominic circled back around to where they had parked. He set his feet down, placed one hand on his hip, and grinned at Corbin.

"See?" he said. "I told you we don't always ride as hard as we did yesterday!"

"That was slower?" Corbin asked. "I thought we made better time today."

"Yeah, well," Dominic said, casting a questioning eye upon Angela, "maybe the time passed quicker for you today."

Corbin could not bring himself to look Dominic in the eye, nor did he dare to look at Angela.

"Yeah," he said. "Going slower made it more fun, I guess."

Raven came walking over from where she and Thomas had parked.

"If there's anything else that we can do to make you feel more welcome," she grunted, "I'm sure Angela and Thomas will trip over each other to make it happen."

"*Raven,*" Dominic said. His tone conveyed neither reproach nor anger; more than anything, he sounded remorseful. Raven shoved her hands into the pockets of her jacket, shook her head in disgust, and started walking briskly toward Clair's.

"You may have guessed by now," Angela whispered, "that Raven didn't want you to join our group."

"I picked up a subtle hint here and there," Corbin replied glumly.

"It's got nothing to do with you," Dominic was quick to point out. "She's just … not on board with the whole thing. You know?"

"She liked the small, intimate group that we had," Angela elaborated. "She had a nickname for us. 'The Four Horsemen,' she called us. She doesn't want to see that change."

"Four Horsemen," Corbin repeated dully. Giving in to a sarcastic impulse, he added: "Any idea which of you is which?"

"Only thing I know for sure is," Thomas said, walking up alongside of Dominic, "Donny here ain't Famine."

Thomas proceeded to pat Dominic on the stomach with an air of solemnity. Dominic glared at him said:

"This is why your mother doesn't love you."

"Not the way your mamma does."

"Bite me."

"Take a shower fist, and then we'll talk about it."

To Corbin, their gentle bickering sounded like it was coming from somewhere far away. Less than a minute ago, he had felt like he belonged with them. Suddenly, he had been reminded of the fact that he did not fit in anywhere, and he probably never would.

"I don't want to ruin what you have here," Corbin finally said.

"You won't!" Angela objected miserably. "If she's got a problem with you riding with us—"

"She'll come around," Thomas said, addressing Dominic rather than Corbin. "Another week or so—a month at the most—and she'll have come to terms with it, and you two can get back to the way things were."

Corbin found himself caught off guard by this statement. Thomas seemed to be implying that there was something between Dominic and Raven, though he had not picked up on any chemistry between the two of them. The concept left him further confused as to why Dominic seemed so eager to welcome him into their midst when it was clearly causing tension between himself and Raven.

"Yeah," Dominic grunted. "Yeah, she'll come around. Don't worry about it, Wendell. The rest of us want you to ride with us, and Raven will warm up to you. Just give her some time."

The remaining three of the Four Horsemen started to walk away from Corbin, toward the general store. Corbin followed, though his heart was heavy and his mind was swimming with troubled thoughts.

There was a man standing in the parking lot off to the left with his back toward them wearing a brown, knee-length coat with a faux fur-lined collar. Corbin was surprised to see anyone wearing a coat on such a hot day, but then he realized that the approximately thirty-year-old man was probably homeless. His long, greasy hair and beard and overall disheveled appearance bore testament to that fact, and Corbin figured that he kept the coat on his person through all seasons because it was one of the few things that he owned.

The homeless man turned around, and Corbin felt a chill run down his spine. The man's face was haggard and deeply lined, and his nose reminded Corbin of a bird's beak. His lips were cracked, narrow, and bluish, and there was something uncannily wrong about his eyes. They were of a strange, watery green coloration, and it seemed to Corbin that the man was looking through them rather than at them.

Those are the eyes of a dead man, Corbin thought. Any feelings of pity that he might have initially felt were replaced by abhorrence, and he tore his gaze away from the man.

"Hello, sweetling," the man croaked. To his horror, Corbin realized that those deathly eyes had become fixed upon Angela and that the unkempt stranger had started shuffling toward her. Angela kept her head down and quickened her pace, her mouth agape and her face reddening, and the homeless man lengthened his strides in an effort to overtake her.

"Let her be, man!" Thomas pleaded without looking at the man.

"Where ya going?" the man called after Angela, seemingly hurt by her lack of response. "I want to talk to you!"

"You heard him." Dominic's tone was calm but authoritative, and Corbin saw that he had set himself between Angela and the homeless man. The man stopped walking, his eyes bulging with confusion and his mouth opening and closing as if he were attempting to remember how to speak.

Dominic turned and followed Thomas inside. Corbin was right behind him, but before he reached the door, he heard the homeless man call after them:

"Yeah, you go on, then! Forget about me. Everybody else has!"

Just inside the door, Angela was standing with her back to Corbin, and he saw that she was trembling. Thomas laid a comforting hand on her arm and said:

"I'm sorry that happened."

"I hate Devland," she sobbed. "I hate it here!"

"I know."

"I just want to get out of here. I just want to get away from everything that…."

She sniffed and shook her head vigorously, struggling to regain her composure. Corbin noticed that Thomas had started to reach for her with his other arm as if to embrace her, but something seemed to hold him back. Corbin looked back through the glass doors, a dark rage beginning to swell inside him. He saw the homeless man slowly making his way toward the sidewalk, swaying and bobbing, transitioning back and forth between sobbing wretchedly, muttering under his breath, and howling at the sky in frustration.

What, he wondered, had that lunatic done to Angela?

"Wendell," Dominic called to him, drawing his eyes away from the homeless man. Dominic gestured with his head toward the refrigerated units where the store kept their soft drinks.

"Come on," he said. "Pick your poison."

Dominic and Thomas each picked out a bottle of Coca-Cola, Raven helped herself to a bottle of A&W Root Beer, and Corbin and Angela both settled on Doctor Pepper. All five of them grabbed orange creamsicle bars as well. After they had paid, true to his word, Thomas allowed Corbin to store his purchases in his backpack.

"Thy pack mule awaits," Thomas said, holding out the pack with a humble bow.

"Thanks," Corbin said as he dropped his items into it.

"Always willing to trip over myself to make you feel welcome," Thomas said, grinning. He zipped up his backpack, patted Corbin on the shoulder, and gave Raven a quick wink. Raven scowled at him and started pedaling her bike to the east, Dominic close behind her. Angela started after them, and then Corbin. Thomas quickly threw his pack over his shoulders and started pedaling after them, managing to cut in front of Corbin before he had reached the sidewalk.

Before long, they took a right turn onto Magnolia Lane, and the trees began to outnumber the buildings and to offer fleeting moments of shade. A few minutes later, they took another right onto Hemlock Drive, which was poorly maintained and surrounded by what was rapidly becoming a forest of loblolly pines, eastern hemlock, and sassafras. They came upon a small paved bridge running across a creek, and it was on the right side of this bridge that they dismounted and stowed their bikes. From there, they hiked up a gentle slope, crested a rise in the earth, and found the waterfall.

The creek that ran under the bridge had eroded away the earth beneath the roots of a towering beech tree, forming a crevasse that went back nearly six feet. Runoff from a stream farther up the hill had carved its way through the leaf-strewn ground and ran down over the roots of the giant beech, sending countless little trickles and dribbles of water raining down across the mouth of the crevasse into the creek below. The trickle of runoff, Corbin surmised, was the "waterfall" that he had heard so much about.

The five of them splashed across the shallow creek and ducked beneath the roots of the beech tree, hurrying to pass through the trickles of water, and crawled to the most comfortable looking spots they could find. Corbin seated himself on a flat bit of ground and leaned his back against the cool, damp earth behind him. Thomas lay on his side against a root on Corbin's left, while Angela sat down on a rock at his right. Just beyond her, Dominic and Raven sat hunched beneath a particularly low part of the ceiling, her right shoulder pressing against an obtrusive rock.

"Well, this is it," Dominic said. "This is the waterfall. What do you think?"

In spite of the confined space, his wet socks, and the water that had dumped down his back on the way in, Corbin found the waterfall to be quite enchanting. The sounds of the outside world were drowned out by the constant gurgling and slapping of water. The air beneath the beech tree was cool, and from time to time, a breeze would come playing across the mouth of the crevasse and wick the sweat off of their faces. What mottled sunlight seeped through the rustling leaves played across the falling trickles of water, casting a lightshow of flickering sunbeams across the earthen walls. To Corbin, as simple as this place was, it felt like something out of a fairytale.

"It's really cool," he said earnestly.

Thomas handed Corbin his creamsicle and Doctor Pepper. Corbin thanked him and tore the wrapper off of the creamsicle. He ran his tongue across its slick, softening edges, catching a few tangy drops of melted orange sherbet. He then took a small bite off of the tip, unearthing sweet vanilla ice cream that was still surprisingly firm.

"What do you think of Devland so far?" Dominic inquired.

The first things that came to Corbin's mind were the creepy homeless man and Angela's declaration that she hated it there. Then, balancing these cons against his newfound freedom and how much happier his parents were, he merely shrugged indifferently.

"It's all right," he said.

"What's it like," Angela asked, "living in Devland's most haunted house?"

Corbin was about to take another bite of his creamsicle. He hesitated a moment, and then he took the bite with another shrug.

"Well, I've heard some of the stories," he said. "They don't bother me too much, though."

"So," Thomas pressed him, "you've been there for three days now, and you haven't seen *anything?*"

"Nothing," Corbin admitted. Then, attempting to imitate the voice and accent of the medium in the nineteen eighty-two film *Poltergeist,* he added: "The house is clean!"

To his disappointment, nobody seemed to get the reference, or at least not to find it amusing.

"So, you're saying that it's all bullshit," Angela muttered, crestfallen. "All of those stories…. You're saying that none of it's true?"

Corbin rotated his creamsicle thoughtfully. He knew that the old Wendell house had become something of a cultural landmark to the people of Devland, and it occurred to him that it might be cruel of him to take that source of wonder away from them. Angela seemed rather heartbroken by his remarks at any rate, so he decided to ease her pain the only way he could think of.

"It's just that," he amended, "I have been having these really weird dreams."

Dominic let out a groan.

"Oh!" Thomas exclaimed delightedly. "We're telling each other about our dreams now? How intimate! Somebody, please hold my hair back while I throw up."

"Shut up, Thomas," Angela scolded him. "You say that these dreams were weird, Corbin? Weird, how?"

Corbin shared his dreams from the past two nights in excruciating detail, and Angela ate up every word he said with an expression that ever shifted between interest and concern. When he had finished, Raven let out an amused scoff.

"That's it?" Raven said. "That's the most 'supernatural' thing that you've experienced in that house?"

Corbin felt embarrassed, and he tried to hide it by taking a hearty swallow of his Doctor Pepper.

"He's not the first person to have had strange dreams in that house," Angela reminded Raven tersely.

"But these dreams are so easy to explain!" Raven countered. "They're nothing but his subconscious trying to make sense of everything that's happened to him since moving to Devland."

Corbin frowned disagreeably.

"How do winged ladies and a pointy-eared boy have anything to do with—"

"Wandering into a dark forest full of strange creatures?" Raven paraphrased cynically. "Obviously, that's symbolic of you moving into a new town full of people and places that you haven't familiarized yourself with yet. The boyish figure that told you that you didn't belong there was the part of your mind that realizes that you don't really fit in with us and that you'd be better off making friends somewhere else."

Corbin stared at his bottle of Doctor Pepper, beginning to feel sick. Though he did not want to accept this explanation, there was a part of him that knew it made sense.

"Really, Raven?" Thomas snapped at her. "Is that where this is—"

"As for the old hag with the box," Raven went on, ignoring Thomas, "I would say that she would have to represent Angela."

"*Angela?!*" Corbin blurted out indignantly. There were so many things that struck him as being wrong with that analysis. He almost came to Angela's defense by pointing out that, if the creature had really represented her, it would have been much more beautiful. He could not, however, bring himself to say such a thing out loud.

"As for the box that she was holding," Raven continued, "that's a little trickier."

"I hardly even noticed the box, though," Corbin argued. "I don't think it was important."

"The fact that you noticed it at all," Angela admitted with an evident measure of reluctance, "together with the way that you said the creature in your dream was so protective of it, indicate that it was, in fact, *very* important. It may well have been the most important part of the dream! Think about it now and tell me: what do you suppose might have been in the box?"

"I have no idea," Corbin said, starting to become irritated by their psychoanalysis and wishing he had not shared his dreams with them in the first place. "You two are doing a great job so far, so how about you tell me what *you* think was in it?"

"Perhaps," Angela suggested coyly, "the box is symbolic of something that you've been hiding from your conscious mind? A secret emotion or desire perhaps?"

Feeling vulnerable and ill at ease, Corbin took another swig from his bottle of Doctor Pepper. As he did so, he considered the implications of Raven's and Angela's theories. The thought of what they suggested made his face flush, and the awkwardness of the moment was only enhanced when, after he had downed the last of his Doctor Pepper, he let out a short yet audible belch.

"In any case," Angela concluded, "there is only one way to be sure of what the box signifies."

"Yeah, and what is that?" Corbin grumbled.

"You have to look inside it," Angela said. "The next time you dream about this passageway in your basement, you have to approach the creature and ask her to show it to you."

Corbin thoughtfully stroked the rim of his now empty Doctor Pepper bottle with his thumb.

"It's not as easy as all that, though," he pointed out. "Like I said, the winged lady was very protective of it. She's not going to just hand it over."

"This is *your* dream!" Angela countered. "Go back into it with the expectation that you can persuade her to give you the box, and she will."

"And if the boy with the pointy ears shows up, or if more of those winged creatures come after me, what then?"

"Close your eyes," Angela instructed, "tell them to go away, and when you've opened your eyes, they will be gone."

Corbin began to scratch at the label on his bottle, reluctantly considering her suggestion.

"You really think that will work?"

"Of course, it will work!" Angela assured him. "They're just dreams, Corbin. Remember?"

Corbin remained at the waterfall for close to an hour after that. Over the course of that time, their conversations covered topics like school, what their parents did, and movies that they had seen. Corbin was the first to leave. Dominic promised to use his backpack to dispose of Corbin's creamsicle wrapper and Doctor Pepper bottle, and Thomas and Angela urged him to come riding with them again the next day. After having said his goodbyes, Corbin recovered his bike, rode back down Hemlock Drive, and was almost at the intersection where Magnolia Lane met up with

Margo Street when he heard the buzz of tires on pavement close behind him.

He looked over his shoulder and saw Raven riding hard, evidently trying to overtake him. Corbin pulled over by the side of the road. His heart sank when, just as he had feared, Raven pulled up beside him and brought her bike to a stop. She sat there for a moment, regarding him with a stern expression on her face.

"What do you want, Raven?" Corbin asked miserably.

"Those guys," Raven said, motioning with her head in the direction they had come from, "they don't like you. They act like they do, but they don't. The best thing that you can do from now on is just stay home."

That having been said, she sped off toward Margo Street, leaving Corbin sitting by the side of the road and seething with anger. Corbin had felt that he was getting along well with Angela, Dominic, and Thomas, and for a little while he had believed that he had a real shot at being permanently accepted into their group. Now, all of his joy and optimism were gone. The entire ride home, he thought about nothing but how much he hated Raven Moore.

After he had made it home, he managed to push his animosity to the back of his mind by fixing his thoughts on his dreams. His father had advised him that there was nothing to be gained by dwelling on them, but from the first night they had slept in that house, Corbin had been driven by an almost instinctive feeling that the dreams were trying to show him something. Furthermore, that morning, Angela had given him something specific to search for. Corbin decided that, should he find himself dreaming about that space between their washing machine and dryer again, he would pass through the icy pool and explore the world beyond it one more time.

Just once more, he told himself. *Once more won't do any harm.*

Chapter Seven
That Which Was Lost

Corbin went to bed that night with little hope of returning to the subterranean forest in his dreams. The more he thought about his discussion with Angela and Raven that afternoon, the more he became convinced that his dreams truly had been brought on by their having moved into a new place. Now that he had talked about the dreams, and in so doing had stripped them of their air of mystique, he doubted if they would ever come back.

This realization was a bittersweet one. There was a certain comfort that came from believing he was no longer going to be summoned into dark forests to be stalked by winged, hissing creatures, but there was also a sense of loss. The dreams had been like a private world of his own, full of magic and horrific wonders. Laying them bare for other people to dissect had ruined that. The magic had died, replaced by the harsh reality that he was just a scared little boy who had trouble sleeping in strange places.

It took him less than an hour to fall asleep that night, and his sleep remained untroubled until about three o'clock in the morning. It was at that time that he found himself sitting upright, listening for the sound of the melody from his previous dreams.

He heard nothing. He got out of bed, took a few steps toward the door, and cocked his head to listen again. Still, he heard nothing, and he decided that some mundane sound—one of his parents coughing in their sleep, or perhaps a passing car—must have awakened him. Corbin turned around, took a single step toward his bed, and then froze. In his bed, tucked under the green and blue quilt with its back turned toward him, was his own body.

Alarmed, he drew in a sharp inhalation of breath. As he did so, the body in his bed gasped slightly and began to stir. Corbin steadied his breathing and tried to slow the hammering of his heart, fearful that he might wake up. To his relief, the body in his bed continued to snore softly, its heavy and undisturbed breathing following a half a beat behind his own.

He went out into the hallway and walked as far as his parents' door. Once more he tried to turn the knob, and again the knob seemed to magnetically repel his hand. He furrowed his brow in annoyance.

This is a dream, he reminded himself. *This is* my *dream, and I can do anything I want!*

With that stubborn thought, he pressed his right shoulder to the door and leaned his weight into it. The door almost seemed to vibrate, causing him to glide across its surface and making his arm prickle in a way that reminded him of when his feet fell asleep. He pressed all of his weight and focused all of his will against the door until the vibrating barrier relented and he lunged through the solid wood.

His father was lying on his back on the right side of the bed. His mother was on the left side, her head tucked close to James's armpit with one arm slung across his chest. At first, it seemed to Corbin as if he were viewing his parents through a refractive lens. He tried to bring his eyes into focus until he comprehended that there were, indeed, two fathers and mothers lying in the bed. Spectral imprints of his parents were hovering less than an inch higher than their material bodies, semitranslucent in appearance and quivering violently. The mouths of these apparitions moved silently and their open eyes rolled back and forth, and the sight of them disturbed Corbin so much that he withdrew through the door without attempting to arouse them.

Feeling slightly disconcerted, Corbin hurriedly made his way toward the stairway, away from his parents' room. The sight of those ghostly images protruding from his parents' bodies made him think of eggs, and of how their smooth, dry surfaces served as mere containers for fragile baby birds with bulging eyes that swam in vats of slimy fluid. He did not like to think about how there might be something wet and alien writhing beneath his parents' skins, nor did he care for the fact that he was starting to compare himself to a baby bird that had broken out of its shell too early, and he resolved to finish his mission and return to his body without further delay.

Corbin slunk down the stairway that led into the kitchen. From there, he passed through the trapdoor, descended into the basement, and knelt down in front of the gap between their washing machine and dryer. He reached forward, tentatively dipped his hand into the icy pool, and at length cast himself forward into its frigid depths.

Once submerged, Corbin was momentarily tempted to see what would happen if he were to try to breathe underwater, but he dared not attempt it for fear that the sensation might wake him. He held his breath as he swam toward the orange glimmer that played across the surface of the pool, and when his head finally broke the surface, he found himself looking down the same cavernous passage that he had dreamed about the night before.

Corbin wrapped his arms across his chest, shivering and trying to rub warmth into his biceps as he limped barefooted across the passageway's jagged and damp floor. He saw where he had pulled the torch out of the wall on the previous night, and beneath it was the small pile of shale-like crumbs that he had dislodged. Before long, he had entered the forest of twisted oaks, and no sooner had he done so than he heard the sound of singing coming from somewhere deeper in the forest.

He quickened his pace, forsaking the orange glow of the torches and venturing out into the more subtle illumination of the suspended braziers, treading gingerly upon the carpet of rotten acorns. He ducked beneath deformed trunks, stubbed his toes on bulging roots, and tripped over low hanging branches in the embers' dim light, but he could tell that he was getting closer to the elusive singer.

Eventually, he came across the torch he had wielded on the previous night. It lay where he had dropped it, still burning with a feeble tongue of flame. Something stirred beside the torch, and Corbin realized that it was another grasshopper, or possibly the same one he had seen on the night before. The oily, glistening insect reared itself up and rustled its wings, regarding Corbin in an evident state of agitation.

"Shut up," Corbin muttered with an impatient wave of his hand, yet he gave the insect a decidedly wide berth and left the torch where it lay. He decided that he was probably better off without it anyway, lest its glow should rob of him of the stealth that the relative darkness provided. Soon, he heard the sound of hissing and of rustling wings coming from the branches overhead. He began to regret not bringing the torch, but he forced himself to press on.

It's just a dream. He forced this thought to the forefront of his mind, clinging to it like a lifeline and using it to push his fears aside. *It's just a dream. Just a dream….*

As he drew closer to the source of the haunting melody, he began to make out more of the words in the song:

> *I crossed the Gardens of the Damned,*
> *Through flailing arms and halls of hands.*
> *Such a long, long way to run,*
> *And what a price I paid.*
> *A trinket, gained;*
> *A treasure, lost.*
> *My mother, pained;*
> *A fortune, tossed.*
> *Should I regret all that I've done,*
> *And choices that I've made?*

At last, in a space between two bent oaks, he saw the creature. It was squatting with its back toward him, stooped over and handling something that remained hidden from Corbin. As he approached, the creature raised its head, turned toward him, and let out a hiss.

"Please!" Corbin cried. "Please, don't go!"

The creature snarled and fluttered its wings, though its features seemed to soften a little. It looked down at the box that it was cradling in its hands and began to absentmindedly tinker with it, caressing it, pressing it, and rocking it back and forth. At length, casually pulling its frayed green shawl tighter over its shoulders with one hand, the creature asked in a raspy voice:

"Are you a ghost?"

Feeling both amused and relieved, Corbin let out a laugh.

"No," he assured her. "I am not a ghost."

"You look like a ghost," the creature said.

"I'm not dead," Corbin argued, though the creature's persistence was starting to make him second-guess the matter. The creature shrugged, seemingly unimpressed by his answer.

"Not all who travel are dead," she replied. She stopped fiddling with the box and gave him a severe look.

"You shouldn't be here. It is not safe, and we have no use for you."

Corbin shifted uncomfortably, reminded of something that Raven had said to him that afternoon.

"Before I go," Corbin said, venturing a few more cautious steps toward the creature, "I would like to ask you about that box that you're holding. May I ask what's inside it?"

"I don't know what's inside it," the creature said. "It's a puzzle box, you see. I have yet to figure out how to open it."

"That's a beautiful necklace." Hoping that praise might help him earn the creature's friendship, Corbin smiled and gestured toward a silver pendant with a smooth, white-and-black marbled stone in the center that was hanging from the creature's neck.

The creature's eyes grew brighter, and a smile crossed her face, revealing a mouthful of sharp, jagged teeth.

"Have you ever seen another like it?" she asked eagerly.

"Never," Corbin gushed. Her smile immediately vanished.

"Did I say something wrong?" Corbin asked.

"This necklace is a replica," the creature lamented. "A replica of a priceless treasure given to me by my mother, which I lost many years ago. When you were so quick to notice it, I was hoping that it was because you had found the original."

Corbin thought hard about what possible interpretation this new element in the dream might hold for him. The theme was simple enough: something important had been lost and replaced with a less worthy substitute. He could not see how this revelation pertained to his relationship with Angela, nor was he convinced any longer that the creature symbolized her at all.

"What's your name?" he asked.

"My name is Lorelei," the creature said. Then, with an air of indifference, she added: "You can call me Lore, if you like."

"My name is Corbin," he introduced himself.

"You're a human?"

"Good eye, Lore."

"I am a fairy," Lorelei told him. "A fairy princess, in fact."

"Well, good for you!" Corbin exclaimed in a voice that was thick with sarcasm. It occurred to him that he had adopted a rather rude tone, but given that this was a dream, he did not feel that it made much of a difference.

"I would be most honored," he went on, "if a princess such as yourself would allow me to assist you in the opening of that puzzle box."

Lorelei squinted at him.

"I don't think you could," she said.

"Can I try?"

The fairy hesitated for a moment, and then, with obvious reluctance, she handed Corbin the puzzle box. Dimensionally, the object was almost a perfect cube, about four inches high and deep and a little over four inches long. Its six surfaces were pocked with a number of panels and pressure points, some of which appeared to rotate and some of which could be pushed inward, and when Corbin rocked the box to-and-fro he heard ball bearings rolling about within its various concealed mechanisms.

He busied himself with the box for a while, fully expecting it to open after a few random rotations and depressions. That was not, however, how it turned out. Seconds turned into minutes, and he stopped making random motions and started trying to memorize which combinations he had already tried so that he might try new ones. He started to become irritated, and he soon began to wonder whether there was a way to open the box at all.

"I told you," Lorelei groaned, evidently having picked up on his frustration. "It's such a difficult riddle. I can only imagine what must be inside it, if its creator invented such a challenging lock to keep it hidden."

Corbin thought that his inability to open the box might hold a symbolic meaning too. Perhaps it represented something that was missing from his life that he would never be able to obtain. He held the box close to his ear and shook it, listening to the tumbling of the ball bearings within.

"What makes you so sure that there's *anything* inside?" he challenged. "For that matter, how do you know it was even meant to be opened? Maybe the whole thing is just … some kind of weird art project."

Lorelei's face twisted into a mask of rage, and she snatched the box out of Corbin's hands.

"Who would dare?!" she shrieked, clutching the box to her breast. "Who would go to the trouble of creating such a marvelous puzzle if it were not meant to be solved? Don't you *dare* tell me that I forsook my mother's necklace for *nothing!*"

The sound of resonant laughter drifted down from the branches above them.

"One must be a great fool," a deep voice taunted, "to cast away something precious in exchange for the unknown."

Corbin looked up, and there, roosting on a branch high above them with its knees gripped tightly to its chest, was the boyish creature in the purple vest that he had seen on the night before. Lorelei bared her teeth, hissed at the creature and fled, her shawl trailing behind her as she disappeared into the shadows. The boyish creature hopped down from the branch, landing in front of Corbin. Remembering Angela's advice, Corbin stood his ground, closed his eyes, and shouted:

"Go away!"

When he opened his eyes, he saw nothing but an empty clearing surrounded by deformed oaks. He let out an uneasy laugh, surprised to find that it had actually worked.

"Now, that's just rude."

The voice came from directly behind Corbin. He spun about and found that the creature was hanging upside down from a tree branch, its face mere inches from his own. Corbin yelped and took a step backward, snagging his foot on a root and falling flat on his back. The creature dropped out of the tree, flipping as it fell so that it landed upright. It then began to pace back in forth in front of Corbin, talking to itself, its green eyes flashing with a dark amusement:

"He came back! Why do they always come back? They get away, and still they come back! Have they nothing better to do? Are they incapable of learning?"

From where Corbin lay, covered in the rancid filth of the rotten acorns that had burst under the weight of his fall, he saw that the creature had a leather satchel draped over its right shoulder and a short sword in a sheath tied to its left hip. At the sight of the sword, Corbin started to forget that he was dreaming, and he felt a cold, gut-wrenching sensation of fear stealing over him.

"Who are you?!" he shouted. He had not intended to sound as indignant as his voice conveyed, but panic had deprived him of his composure. "What do you want?!"

The creature stopped pacing and regarded Corbin thoughtfully, and then its face was split by a mischievous grin.

"One is known as the Frog Catcher." The creature made this announcement with an evident measure of pride, delivering it with a sweeping gesture of his arm and a low bow. The unusual title, coupled with the undue level of pomp with which it had been delivered, was absurd enough to alleviate the greater measure of Corbin's fear.

" 'Frog Catcher,' " Corbin repeated, raising himself into a sitting position. "Do you have an actual name, or do you just … anonymously hunt amphibians?"

The creature turned away from Corbin, a sour expression on its face.

"The Frog Catcher had many things, long ago," the creature muttered. "A name was one such thing."

The Frog Catcher's eyes returned to Corbin.

"The memory is a stain upon the Frog Catcher's soul. To remind him of such things is offensive and dangerous."

Corbin had started to get to his feet. He froze, half-erect, afraid to move under the creature's malevolent gaze. Then, as if a switch had been thrown in his brain, the Frog Catcher's features relaxed and his grin resurfaced.

"As for what the Frog Catcher is," the creature said, pausing to straighten its tattered vest in a vain attempt to appear dignified, "he is an elf. Once, there were one hundred and thirty-four elves, but the noble elven bloodline is no more. Only the Frog Catcher remains. As for what the Frog Catcher wants, there is one thing that he desires above all others, but considering that you are in no fit state to assist him, the Frog Catcher sees no reason for confiding in you. In any case, what the Frog Catcher wants is a curious thing to ask, seeing as you are the one gallivanting about in distant corners of the unknown. So, an elf must ask: who are *you*, and what do *you* want?"

"My name is Corbin Wendell."

"And where does Corbin Wendell come from? Is he from Wakeworld?"

Corbin stared at the elf blankly.

"I'm from Devland," he finally answered. "Morgantown, West Virginia, before that."

"What are these, the Frog Catcher wonders?" the elf muttered, beginning to pace again. "Are these the names of places in Wakeworld?"

Corbin stood with his mouth open, feeling exasperated and confused.

"Is Corbin Wendell sleeping in Devland?!" the elf suddenly shouted at him. "Did Corbin Wendell go walking in a dream, and does he expect to wake up in his bed when all of this is over?!"

Corbin nodded, wondering how he had lost control of the situation and allowed his mind to become so far derailed from its purpose. He was fairly certain that the elf was a part of his own subconscious that was afraid to face whatever symbolic truths were hidden in the fairy's puzzle box, and he suspected that the only way he was going to find answers was to beat the Frog Catcher at his own game.

"Well," the elf said, his smile slowly returning as he spoke, "Corbin Wendell of Wakeworld, allow the Frog Catcher to formally welcome you to the Oakland Forest of the Winterland. An elf must ask, however: Is it your wish to set up house here? Is it your intention to become a permanent, flesh-and-blood resident of the Winterland?"

"I'm just passing through," Corbin assured him. "I was rather hoping to have a look at whatever was inside that box before I left, though."

The Frog Catcher stared at Corbin for a moment. Then a peculiar look came over his face, almost as if a terrible truth had just dawned on him.

"And who put that idea into your head, an elf wonders?" the creature murmured. "Why does a boy think it worth his while to seek out this thing that do not belong to him?"

"Oh, it's a terrible idea," Corbin agreed, attempting to appease the elf. "As soon as this is over, I promise I'll leave as fast as I can. If you could just help me find that fairy! I'd really like to know what's inside—"

"You have not answered my question, boy," the Frog Catcher snapped at him, his green eyes flashing menacingly. "Now, tell me truly: why does Corbin Wendell of Wakeworld seek Princess Lorelei's puzzle box?"

"The box is.... It's why I'm here!" Corbin explained annoyedly. "I don't know why I keep dreaming about this place, or what it all means, but I believe that box may hold the answers that I'm looking for. Finding out what's inside the box may be the only way I'll ever understand the meaning behind all of this!"

The Frog Catcher blinked at Corbin in evident confusion, and then he visibly relaxed and let out a hearty laugh.

"The box is nothing!" the elf said, his eyes betraying what might have been relief. "You *know* nothing! You merely happened upon this place through a deplorable turn of fate, and the box was one of the first things you saw here, so you naturally assumed that it held some sort of significance. Allow an elf to explain something to you, boy: your obsession with that wooden enigma is folly. 'The meaning behind all of this,' indeed! There is no *meaning* behind any of it. Of all the places in the Winterland into which you might have blindly stumbled too! You had to turn up here, so close to the devil's lair. So dangerously close! His homunculi's eyes do not seek after flesh-and-blood creatures like the Frog Catcher, but they are ever searching for ghosts. Even now, he may be coming!"

"Who may be coming?" Corbin asked, beginning to feel uneasy once more.

The Frog Catcher cocked his head to one side and started to glance about, sniffing at the air. Suddenly, he lunged forward, grasped Corbin by both shoulders, and pulled him so close that their faces almost touched. Corbin squirmed uncomfortably, the sour and almost acidic odor of the Frog Catcher's breath wafting over him, smelling similar to how Corbin imagined spoiled spaghetti sauce might smell.

"Are you afraid, boy?" the elf asked.

Corbin's breathing had become shallow, and he found that he could not bring himself to answer.

"You should be afraid," the Frog Catcher urged him. "For your own sake, you *must* be afraid! Soon, it may be too late. Soon, you may never be able to wake up again, no matter how much fear is in your heart nor how much pain is in your flesh! The Frog Catcher begs—"

The Frog Catcher fell silent, his attention drawn by something behind Corbin. Corbin tore free of the elf's grasp, turned around, and saw a five-inch-long, green Luna moth sitting on the branch of a nearby tree. The Frog Catcher let out a hiss and ran away, leaping over branches and darting between trunks until he had disappeared from view. Corbin stared after the elf for a moment, bewildered, and then he looked back at the unassuming moth.

A few seconds later, Corbin became aware of an eerie whooshing sound, like the sound of many leaves stirring in a strong breeze. The moth lifted off of the branch and began to flutter, and Corbin was seized by a primal, thoughtless panic. Fear came crashing over him like an icy wave, dimming his vision and drawing the strength out of his legs until he fell to his knees. The trees, the hanging braziers, and the ground upon which he had fallen seemed to vibrate with the hint of shadowy things that lay just beyond his vision, ready to reach out and drag him away into horrors that no mortal mind could hope to comprehend. A twenty-foot-wide, undulating shadow appeared in the distance, sweeping through the trees like a cloud of smoke.

"*Go away!*" Corbin screamed the protective mantra once more, but this time he did not dare to close his eyes. He cowered on his hands and knees before the approaching mass, whimpering with every exhalation. Hundreds of Luna moths passed through the trees into the clearing. They began to cluster together and collide, bashing themselves into a whirlwind of dusty debris and blood that finally compressed together and took on the form a single, slender, seven-foot-tall humanoid being.

The being was dressed in an ankle-length trench coat made out of irregularly shaped patches of black leather. It wore a five-inch-wide leather belt across its waist, and there was a two-foot-long sickle clipped to the belt over its left hip. It wore leather boots and gloves, had a black cotton newsboy cap perched on its bald head, and had no face. The front of its skull bore nothing but a smooth, round veil of waxy-looking skin with blue veins pulsing beneath the surface.

Voices sighed through the forest, seemingly coming out of the trees and the ground, overlapping and slightly out of sync with one another, yet all speaking the same words:

"You seem to be lost."

"Please!" Corbin screamed, convulsing under the weight of the unnatural fear that had taken hold of him.

"Hush, now," the gentle, almost soothing voices echoed through the forest. The creature stepped forward, stooped down, and closed its left hand into a fist around Corbin's jaw. Its thumb slid between Corbin's teeth, digging into the soft tissue beneath his tongue, and the knuckle of its index finger pressed into Corbin's throat. Corbin cried out in agony as he was yanked to his feet so forcefully that his jaw was nearly dislocated.

"Be still," the voices said, and the creature held Corbin so that his toes barely touched the ground. Pain began to spread across the right side of Corbin's face, radiating like fingers of molten lead that pulsed outward with every beat of his heart.

"Don't be afraid. This will only hurt a little bit."

The creature thrust its right arm forward like a spear, driving its hand deep into Corbin's chest with a ripe cracking sound. Corbin let out a strangled cry, and his entire body shuddered. The pain in his face became less pronounced and the light of the braziers seemed to grow dim, and he knew that he was on the verge of blacking out. The faceless entity tore something out of his ribcage with a wet sucking sound, and then he allowed Corbin to collapse onto the ground.

The pain in Corbin's chest and jaw had become barely noticeable, and he was only vaguely aware of the needling of the cracked acorn shells beneath him as he weakly stirred upon the forest floor. The world around him was receding into shadows, but he could still make out the shape of what the faceless man had torn out of his chest: a squirming, transparent clump of ghostly white flesh with a number of tendrils extending from it.

"*Yes,*" the voices in the trees and ground hissed in satisfaction. As the world around Corbin faded into utter darkness, that last thing he saw was the part of himself that had been stolen writhing within the monster's grasp, wrapping itself around and writhing between the creature's fingers as if trying to escape.

"*Perfect.*"

Corbin felt himself being yanked backward, and then he found himself lying in his bed in the same position in which he had seen himself sleeping. He sat up with a hoarse scream and instinctively grabbed at the spot where his chest had been cracked open. There was no wound to be found, but his chest felt cold. His whole body felt cold. His eyes roved across the room, seeking out the familiar sights of his bedside lamp, the *Return of the Jedi* poster, and his green and blue quilt, but their familiarity provided no comfort.

He got out of bed and walked out into the hall, desperate for a drink of water. His legs felt numb and heavy, and he felt so disconnected from his surroundings that he was not sure if was awake or still dreaming. He went down into the kitchen, took a glass out of the cupboard, and began to fill it with water from the sink. The water foamed and roiled as it fell into the glass, making a sound that seemed distant and unreal.

Corbin looked around him. Everything about the kitchen was exactly the way he remembered it, but he felt as if something had changed; something subtle that he had yet to pin down. Everything he saw and heard felt as if it belonged in a dream rather than in the real world. Then something cold began to rush over his fingers, and he realized that his glass was overflowing.

He turned the faucet off and raised the water toward his lips, but his trembling hand lost control of the glass and it fell to the floor and shattered. His bare feet were drenched in cold water and bombarded by flying shards of glass, and he turned toward the trapdoor in terror. He half expected to see the faceless man come charging up the steps to investigate, but nobody came.

He shook his head vigorously and rubbed at his eyes. He was still desperately thirsty, but he could not be bothered to fill another glass. He walked into the sitting room and sat down on one of the couches. For hours he sat and stared into space, trying to figure out precisely what was wrong with the world that he had woken up into, occasionally touching his hand to the spot on his chest where the faceless man had reached inside him. He was still sitting there at five o'clock, when he heard his parents' alarm going off upstairs.

Chapter Eight
Incompletion

It might have taken Corbin's mother ten minutes to come downstairs. It might have taken half a lifetime. Each second seemed to linger, digging in its heels and refusing to allow the next to be born. Corbin did not know what was wrong with him. He was aware that he felt quite different, but aside from a general dulling of his senses and a heavy feeling in his gut, he felt none of the symptoms that he had come to associate with being sick.

Corbin suffered from neither a fever, nor cramps, nor a sore throat. He dreaded the thought of having to explain how he felt to his parents when he was so far from understanding it himself, even though he longed for their presence and the imagined comfort that it would bring. The seconds continued to march ponderously onward, slowly and deliberately, until his mother finally appeared on the stairway across the dining room.

She was wearing her beige robe and her hair was tousled. She passed directly into the kitchen, seemingly without noticing Corbin. He heard the patter of her bare feet come to an abrupt halt and there was a sharp inhalation, and he deduced that she must have discovered the shattered glass. Corbin groaned inwardly. He had forgotten about the glass.

Emily hurried back into the dining room. Her eyes darted about until they came to rest on Corbin, and she began to hurry toward him.

"What happened?" she asked. She lowered her gaze to his feet, evidently worried that he might have trodden upon the glass. "Are you all right?"

"I'm sorry," Corbin replied dully. "I forgot about the glass."

Emily studied him, her concern clearly written on her face, and then she placed a hand to his forehead to check for a fever. The feel of his brow did not seem to satisfy her.

"Are you sick?" she asked.

Corbin did not know how to answer that. He did not believe that he was sick in any sense of the word that he was familiar with, but he knew that he was not altogether well either. It had only been a dream. A dream that was somehow more than a dream, in which a monster had torn a piece of who he was right out of him. Yes, he decided; he was sick, just not in any way that he could hope to make her understand.

"I'm fine, Mom," he lied. "I just had a bad dream."

Her brow became furrowed.

"About the old women in the basement?"

Corbin did not look at his mother. The old, winged women had been in his dream, but there had been so much more than that, and this dream had been so much worse than the others. At length, he merely said:

"Yes."

James came down the stairs next, tucking his white dress shirt into his pants as he walked. He gave Emily and Corbin a perplexed stare and glanced toward the kitchen, presumably checking to see whether his breakfast was on the stove or not. His eyes dropped as if magnetically drawn to the shattered glass on the floor, and he looked back at Emily.

"Why is there broken glass just lying—"

"It was an accident," Emily told him. "I was about to clean it up, but Corbin isn't feeling well."

"Yeah?" James inquired, approaching them. "What is it, Corbin? What hurts?"

Corbin did not know how to answer that. Nothing really hurt. In fact, he did not feel much of anything. He usually felt something: happiness or sorrow; contentedness or anxiety. Now all he felt was emptiness, as if he had somehow been reduced.

"Just tired, mostly, I guess," he said.

"How long have you been awake?" James asked.

Corbin shrugged.

"A couple hours, I guess."

"He had another nightmare," Emily added in a whisper.

James frowned. He closed his eyes and shook his head.

"Corbin," he said, speaking in the tone of a man who is shouldering an unwelcome burden, "we need you to stop."

Corbin blinked at his father in confusion.

"Stop making such a big thing out of these nightmares," James went on. "We don't want you getting some sort of a rush from talking about them, or for you to start feeling like they give you a chance to be the center of attention. Did you tell those kids you ride your bike with about these dreams too?"

Corbin was struck speechless for a moment. Telling his friends about his dreams had not felt wrong, and he still did not fully understand why it would have been, but under his father's demanding gaze, his stomach began to turn with a sickening feeling of guilt. His mother stood with her head bowed and her hands shoved into the pockets of her robe, her eyes unwaveringly fixed on some point between James and Corbin.

"They asked me," Corbin began meekly, "if I had seen anything weird in this house."

"Jesus, Corbin!" James groaned. "I already told you yesterday: you have to stop dwelling on these dreams! And now, what? I find out that you've been telling them to a bunch of kids that you barely even know?"

"Stop it, James," Emily said.

James stared at his wife, bewildered.

"Stop what?"

"There's no reason for you to be so hard on him."

"I wasn't being hard on him!" James said. "I just don't want him telling people about the dreams. They're not campfire stories."

"Our son is sick!" Emily spat at him. "And all you seem to care about is what gossip might come of it."

James squirmed agitatedly.

"Gossip can lead to a lot of harm in a small town like this," he said. "And what are you even talking about, our son being sick? Corbin! Are you sick?"

Corbin did not answer. He stared gloomily at his right hand, scratching at the cuticle of his thumb with the nail of his index finger.

"Yeah, I thought so," James said. "He had a *nightmare*, Em. Kids *have* nightmares. There's no reason to let the whole town know the gory details. You know my family already has a reputation here. I don't think you understand, or appreciate, how hard it was for me to even come back here."

"You *chose* this!" Emily reminded him, crossing her arms defensively. "You could have applied at any medical practice you wanted, but you decided to settle for a fast-track to success from your brother. You want me to *appreciate* that? Like the way you appreciated *me* when I had to work double shifts in every department store and shoe outlet in Morgantown to pay for your schooling? You talk about your life like it's some—"

"You knew what you signed up for!" James snapped at her. "You'd work side jobs and pay the bills; I'd go to school and try to make something of myself. If you'd actually gone to college—hell, if you'd actually focused on getting decent grades when you were in high school—then maybe you wouldn't have had to settle for—"

"You really want to go there?!" Emily shot back at him indignantly. "My grades were *outstanding*—my whole *life* was outstanding—before you—"

"What?" James cried. "Before I *what?* What did I do that was so terrible that it destroyed your otherwise perfect—"

"I could have done *anything!*" she said, and for a moment, she looked as if she were about to cry. "I could have *been* anything, and I threw it all away to pave the way for you and your—"

"Then why *didn't* you?!" James demanded. "If going back to school and making something of myself was so easy, then why didn't *you* give it a try?!"

Corbin's heartbeat had become a rapid patter in his chest, and his entire body felt cold. His parents were fighting again. In spite of their having moved to a new town—in spite of his father's new career and the promise of a new life—things were beginning to fall apart again. His mouth felt dry, and his stomach was starting to churn so harshly that he felt as if he might vomit.

"I won't talk about the dreams!" he cried. His parents looked at him, shocked, almost as if they had forgotten that he was there.

"I won't talk about the dreams," he repeated. "You'll never have to hear about them again."

James groaned and ran his fingers backward through his short hair, causing it to stand up in a manner which might have been comical under other circumstances.

"Don't say that, Corbin," James pleaded. "It's not that we don't want to hear about them. You can talk to us about anything. We just want you to stop *thinking* about them so much. We just want them to stop."

"They will," Corbin eagerly assured him. "No more bad dreams. I promise."

Corbin meant it. If he found himself waking up to the sound of singing or to anything else ever again, he was not going to get up to investigate or even to use the bathroom; he was going to simply lie back down and wait until his parents' alarm went off.

He no longer cared about what might have been inside the fairy's puzzle box. He had decided that it was time for his nights of chasing after phantom voices and exploring strange new worlds to come to an end.

James left for work that morning later than usual, but not so late that he would fail to be at Uncle Kurt's medical practice on time. His departure was graceful enough, but Corbin could tell that the taste of his parents' argument was still sour in their mouths and that both of them felt that the other owed them an apology. After finishing his breakfast, Corbin retreated to the chair in the living room, where he sat in silent reflection for over an hour.

At about a quarter past seven, he was aroused from his dismal musings by the sound of laughter and chattering coming from outside. He crept over to the window overlooking Butterwort Street and gapped the venetian blinds with one finger, spacing them just enough to confirm that Dominic, Thomas, and Angela were circling in front of his house, riding around each other in an ever-changing series of loops.

Corbin gently allowed the blinds to fall back into place and returned to the comfort of the living room chair. He sat in a state of heart-pounding suspense, his fingernails scratching at and digging into the arms of the chair, hoping that the three riders would go away. Their laughter continued and their jovial shouts were so loud that Corbin feared his mother would come downstairs to investigate and that, upon doing so, might urge him to go outside and play. Corbin did not want to play, nor did he want to have to try to explain to them how he was somehow sick without actually being sick.

After what felt like an eternity—in truth, it was probably no more than ten minutes—the riders left, the sound of their tumult fading into the distance with them. Corbin felt as if he could breathe again, though only barely. He still felt like a saltwater fish in a freshwater aquarium, and he had no way of knowing whether he had somehow swum into the wrong tank or if it was he, the fish, who had been transformed.

Corbin sought solace from Mary Shelley's *Frankenstein* for a while, but after every few paragraphs he realized that he was merely skimming over the words without making any effort to comprehend what they were saying. Each time he caught himself doing this, he forced himself to back up and reread the parts that had eluded him, but he found focusing on the words to be nearly impossible. With an aching heart, he came to terms with the fact that he was not capable of enjoying books anymore. There was simply not enough of him left; the faceless man had torn away too much of him.

That was just a dream, Corbin reminded himself, his fists clenching with rage at his own stupidity. *You're still here. You're still you! Nothing that happened last night was real.*

Despite this lackluster epiphany, Corbin elected to give up on books for the day. He returned *Frankenstein* to the shelf without bothering to mark his place or take note of which page he had left off on, opting to settle for the mindless stimulation of rewatching their DVD of *The Others*.

Somehow, the movie seemed slightly different than Corbin remembered it. There was nothing specific that he could readily say had been altered; it just felt, for want of a better word, "flat." Not in a dimensional sense, but in the way a half-drunk bottle of soda left sitting overnight goes flat. In that same sense, the entire house felt "flat." It was as if every sound had been muffled and every light had been dimmed, though, the more Corbin scrutinized his surroundings, the more he was inclined to believe that they were exactly the same. It was more like his mind had become slower at processing things; as if he had somehow been rendered immune to whatever beauty the world had once offered.

Corbin cradled his head in his hands, closed his eyes, and whispered:

"Go away."

He opened his eyes, and nothing had gone away or changed. The world remained flat, and he was still broken.

"I want to wake up now." He sobbed. "If this is a dream, I want to *wake up now!*"

Those last three words came out as a desperate cry, but it seemed that neither his mother nor anybody else had heard them. The movie played on, a meaningless collage of images and sounds. His heart continued to throb in his chest, his lungs continued to involuntarily draw and expel breath, and the life that Corbin had woke into clung to him like a foul stench that could not be washed off.

The conversation around the dinner table in the Wendell house that evening was polite but forced. Corbin could tell that both of his parents were trying to put their best foot forward and leave that morning's argument in the past, but there was a lingering tension in the air, like a cloud of noxious gas that required nothing but a tiny spark to set it off. There was something else in the air as well, Corbin realized: there was an undercurrent of fear hidden just beneath the surface of his parents' forced smiles. Something had them scared, and Corbin was fairly certain that it was him.

"You feeling better, Corbin?" Emily finally asked the question that had clearly been on both of their minds. His parents avoided looking directly at him at this point, evidently attempting to hide their concern behind a facade of casual interest, but Corbin noticed how their movements slowed and how his father inclined one ear toward him.

"I'm fine," Corbin answered as honestly as he knew how. After all, was he not fine? Losing focus and being unhappy did not equate to being unwell. "I just need one good, solid night of uninterrupted sleep. I'll be okay after that."

James and Emily exchanged cautious glances that might have conveyed a measure of apprehension. James resumed the act of tearing apart a baked potato with his fork, smashing it and prodding at a slab of butter that was reluctantly melting into the white, crumbly tuber. He cleared his throat once, and then he announced:

"You know what I think we should do? Take a drive out to the Veteran's State Park on Saturday. We could rent a few kayaks; row around Lake Blackshear for a few hours; maybe throw some lines in the water."

Corbin remembered that his father had mentioned Lake Blackshear at Uncle Kurt's house. Corbin deduced that his father had enjoyed the lake as a child and that, in his mind, it was only natural to assume that Corbin was bound to enjoy it, as well. In truth, the prospect of having to get in a boat and row around a lake sounded rather daunting. The mere task of shoveling forkfuls of baked potato into his mouth, chewing, and swallowing had become daunting. Still, Corbin knew that his father meant well, and he was hopeful that he might feel up to it after a couple of nights of dreamless slumber.

"That sounds like fun," Corbin said, trying to sound more excited than he was.

"The lake really is something to see," James went on enthusiastically. "It's not a natural lake. It's manmade, but you wouldn't know it from the size of it! One of the coolest things, I think, is that there's cypress trees growing out of the middle of it. When they first made the lake, they thought that the trees would eventually fall down and die, but they're still growing out there. It's the most bizarre thing, seeing treetops poking out of the middle of a lake! Like something out of a fairy tale, you know?"

Corbin did not much care for this analogy. Lately, his whole life had started to feel like a fairy tale, and he wondered whether there had been any death-defying trees growing in the middle of the lake prior to his most recent nightmare.

"In any case," James said, turning his attention to Emily, "I think it would do Corbin good to get out of the house and have a bit of fun. I think it would do all of us some good."

Emily nodded thoughtfully.

"I suppose it might," she admitted.

"Maybe we'll catch some fish," James added dreamily. "Maybe our kayaks will run afoul of a submerged tree and we'll have to swim back to shore. Either way, how exciting!"

This attempt at humor, if it was one, landed flat, garnering nothing more than a forced guffaw from Emily.

"Yeah," she finally said. "Yeah, I suppose it would do us all some good."

They did not discuss the lake any further that evening, but Corbin believed that his parents were decided on the matter. Not that it made any difference, by his way of thinking. Either a couple of nights of uninterrupted sleep would mend his damaged mind, or they would not. If they did, a trip to the lake would be unnecessary; if they did not, Corbin feared that there was not a vacation destination in the world that could give him hope.

Corbin went to bed a little after eight o'clock that night. He was determined to catch up on the sleep that he had missed out on since having moved into that house, but above all else, he was determined not to have any more nightmarish adventures.

He wondered what would happen if he heard Lorelei's song in the night and refused to go after it. Would he spend the rest of the night in a state of awareness, neither asleep nor awake? Would he hover halfway out of his body as he had seen his parents doing, quivering and rolling his eyes and snapping his teeth until morning? He decided that it did not matter, as anything would be better than risking another encounter with the faceless man.

As exhausted as he was, it did not take Corbin long to fall asleep. The instant he had done so, he felt the all-too-familiar sensation of a cord on his spine being yanked backward, and he woke up on a cold and wet stone floor. He sat up and looked around in astonishment. He was lying in the center of a roughly ten-foot-wide by ten-foot-deep room comprised of stones and mortar. In front of Corbin was a door made out of heavy iron bars. On the other side of the door, lurking in the shadows and making odd clucking noises in its throat, was a creature no larger than a child.

The naked, feminine form had withered breasts and yellowish skin that was tightly stretched over a bulging, deformed skeleton. The creature had an elongated face with sharp teeth and a flat nose, and a few sparse strands of long, golden hair dangled from its otherwise bare scalp. Its huge, bat-like ears made up nearly half of the volume of its head, and it had a rotten, oozing eyeball in its right eye socket. The left socket was empty, and there was a scar running down that side of the creature's face.

The creature began to dance about in excitement, flailing its arms and causing a chain around its neck to clink and sway.

"It's awake, Master!" the creature rasped eagerly.

Corbin sat huddled and shivering on the damp floor, staring in revulsion at the form that was contorting and bobbing about on the other side of the door. Then he felt a pair of massive, gloved hands come gently to rest on his shoulders, and a familiar chorus of voices that seemed to come out of the rocks and the air sang out:

"Rise and shine, child! Did you sleep well?"

Chapter Nine
Flesh and Blood

The faceless man's right hand started to stroke the side of Corbin's neck, sending a chill down his spine.

"I don't want you to be afraid," the faceless man said. "I want us to be friends. I believe that, if we can come to trust one another, we might be able to help each other."

"*Help!*" the creature outside the door shrieked with a deranged laugh. "We *help* each other!"

"Be quiet, Riddle!" the faceless man shouted, and the creature cowered away from him with a whimper.

"Allow me to introduce myself," the faceless man resumed, tousling Corbin's hair as he stepped around him. Corbin was beginning to feel faint, and he found that he could only draw breath in short, rapid gasps.

"My name is Klein," the faceless man announced with a polite bow. "And you are?"

"My name," Corbin forced the words out of his throat, "is Corbin."

In a desperate bid to sound important, hoping that it would make the faceless man less inclined to hurt him, he added:

"My father is a doctor. My father is Doctor James Wendell."

"Ah!" Klein exclaimed in evident amusement. "A *doctor,* is he? Well, that's just wonderful! I'm a doctor of sorts too. So, tell me, child: Have you been having trouble sleeping? Or bad dreams? Or inexplicable moments of passing insanity?"

Corbin tried to stammer out a reply, but Klein shushed him.

"If I am to help you," Klein continued softly, beginning to pace in tight circles around Corbin, "I must first give you an examination. Now, I want you to open your mouth, stick out your tongue and say … *AAAH!*"

Klein's scream echoed through the room and reverberated inside Corbin's head, wrenching a cry of pain from him.

"Louder!" Klein urged. "Say it! Say *AAAH!*"

Corbin pressed his hands over his ears and screwed his eyes shut, and then he screamed.

"Very good!" Klein praised. "There! Didn't that make you feel better?"

Corbin let out a nearly inaudible whimper.

"Excellent!" Klein said, evidently pleased with this response. "Now, let's get down to business, shall we? You are from Wakeworld, are you not?"

"Yes," Corbin said, vaguely recalling something that the Frog Catcher had said to that effect. "I believe so."

"How did you come to be here?"

"I was dreaming."

"And in this dream, you found a doorway?"

"Yes."

"Where was this doorway exactly?"

"It was in the basement of our new house, between a washing machine and a dryer."

"Yes, yes," Klein went on impatiently, "and where did this doorway between a washing machine and a dryer take you? At what location, precisely, did you enter the Winterland?"

"A pool of water. I found myself swimming in a pool near the forest, at the end of a tunnel."

"The Pool of the Princess's Tears?" Klein asked, a tremor of anger in his voice.

"I don't know what it's called," Corbin said. "It was at the end of a stone passageway lit by torches. When I followed it, it led out into the forest where you found me last night."

"*Liar!*" Klein's many voices roared. Corbin winced and drew back, and the faceless formed stomped toward him in a state of fury. "Liar and conspirator! I do not know why you

Wakeworlders keep coming here, or why you are willing to go to such lengths to deceive me, but I have already checked on that version of the story. There is no passage between worlds in the Pool of the Princess's Tears."

"Maybe it wasn't the Pool of the Princess's Tears!" Corbin cried miserably. "I don't know the name of the pool! I just know that it was a small pool of water at the end of—"

"There is no other pool at the end of a tunnel that connects to the Oakland Forest," Klein countered. "You are not the first to tell me this story about a doorway in that pool, but there is not, nor has there ever been, anything there."

That having been said, Klein exploded into a cloud of Luna moths. Corbin fell prostrate on the ground and covered his face. The moths seemed to fill the entire room, the wind of their rapidly beating wings stinging his eyes and droning maddeningly against his ears. The moths passed through the door and into the hall, at which point they came back together and took on the form of a faceless man once more.

"Do not dare to imagine that you can conceal the truth from me, Wakeworlder," Klein warned Corbin. He took hold of the chain around the one-eyed creature's neck and began to scratch its head, and the creature moaned and nuzzled Klein's leg. "My homunculi's eyes never rest. From now on, every time you fall asleep and dream of your precious Wakeworld, their eyes will gaze upon your fragment, which will in turn gaze after you. In time, I will find where your path intersects with those of the other Wakeworlders. Eventually, through you or through another, I will find the entrance through which you all come. If you are not the one to give me what I desire, or if your fragment dies before I have what I want, you will wish that your mother had ripped you out of her belly with a coat hanger."

Klein gave the chain a sharp tug and began moving off to the right, walking with long and elegant strides. The creature called

Riddle purred and clucked after him, hunched over, walking with a peculiar three-limbed gait that required regular assistance from one arm or the other. A small measure of Corbin's fear lifted after the two entities were out of sight, and he sat back up and began to look around his small prison.

The only light came from distant flames burning somewhere out in the hallway. The barred door appeared to be the only way in or out. There were broken pieces of stone ranging from the size of his fist to the size of gravel littering the floor, and he could make out a number of dark stains of what he was inclined to believe was blood.

Directly above him, hanging from a short chain fastened to the ceiling, was a birdcage, the door to which had a lock built into it. Corbin stood up to examine the cage, and inside it he saw what looked like a bizarre wickerwork doll woven out of twisted ropes of rotting flesh. The two-foot-tall, slouched creation seemed to have been woven around a meager skeleton consisting of a spine, four ribs, and a few other curiously positioned bones. The grotesque creation was topped off by a crude leather helmet shaped like a bird's head.

Impossible as it seemed, the doll appeared to be alive. From time to time, one of the wing-like protrusions woven out of its shoulders would twitch, and its helmeted head regularly rocked from side to side while producing wet, nasal sounding chortles. Between its ribs was a forest green glass sphere about as large as a tennis ball over which was draped was a dark, slick blob that looked rather like a slowly pulsating liver. Something was stirring within the glass sphere, and a sensation of dread crept over Corbin when he recognized it as the piece of himself that Klein had torn out of his chest on the previous night.

The white, spectral fragment struggled within the confines of the glass sphere with abrupt movements that reminded Corbin of a mosquito larva. Its tentacle-like extensions were twitching like the fingers of a tiny, twisted white hand. Corbin looked down at his chest, and he saw a four-inch-long, moist, vertical wound where Klein's hand had speared into him.

Corbin's thoughts were interrupted by the sound of a wet, prolonged cough. Across the hall from his prison was another cell, and on the far side of it Corbin saw a pair of bare, withered legs. The rest of the form was cloaked in darkness.

"Who's there?!" Corbin called out.

"Leave me alone," a throaty voice replied, and the words were followed by another chorus of coughs.

Corbin walked over to the door that stood between himself and the hallway. It was held in place by a strong-looking lock and three hinges that were sunken into a frame of stone and mortar. He rattled the door, but all of its bars appeared to be quite sturdy. He heard a number of shrill cries coming from off in the distance, seemingly in response to the commotion that he had made.

He warily backed away from the door, and he soon began to hear a rapid series of clucking sounds and the patter of feet approaching from his left. Seconds later, a male version of whatever manner of creature Riddle had been stepped out in front of the door. The creature's body was naked and withered, its yellow skin clinging to bones that seemed to be almost devoid of flesh.

The creature's oozing, ruptured blue eyes stared vacantly at Corbin. It clucked in its throat a few times, and then it spoke:

"It must be quiet! It must not disturb our master."

The creature then galloped back in the direction from which it had come, utilizing the same hunched-over, three-limbed gait that the creature called Riddle had used.

Corbin stood still for a long while, uncertain of what he should do. His eyes swept the room, reaffirming that there was no way out aside from the locked and barred door. He began to walk around, looking for something that he might have missed, or rather hoping that the dream would change and that something would simply appear. Periodically, the wickerwork bird in the cage would twitch or let out a faint grunt, which only served to compound Corbin's desperation.

Hours passed, during which time Corbin became increasingly aware of how cold he was. He alternated between pacing across the wet stone floor and sitting down upon it, at which point his rust-colored pajamas would soak up its moisture and further add to his wretchedness. From time to time, he would close his eyes and open them again, hoping that he might wake up. He never did. As time went on, he resorted to increasingly desperate measures, such as pinching or slapping himself or punching the walls until his knuckles bled, but he never woke.

At length, Corbin collapsed into a corner, shivering. His knuckles were split and throbbing, and his right wrist was beginning to swell. He was starting to wonder if every night was going to be like this for the rest of his life. Perhaps, he speculated further, he had died in his sleep, and this was what it was like to be dead. He shrank against the wall, allowing the pain, cold, and hopelessness to swallow his soul.

"*Please!*" he finally cried out to no one in particular. "Please, *help me!* I want to go home!"

He heard laughter coming from the cell across the hall.

"Yes, that's it!" the unseen prisoner taunted. "Call for help! They all do, at first. One day, somebody will heed your cries. God help you when they do."

Corbin got to his feet and sprinted across the room, practically flinging himself against the bars.

"Keep talking to me!" Corbin begged. "Please! I have to know what's happening to me!"

The shadowy figure laughed cruelly, and then his laughter was cut short by another fit of coughing. After close to a minute of gut-wrenching hacking sounds, the voice replied:

"What is happening to you, boy, is that you have been caught like a fly in a web. Now you, like the rest of us, face an eternity of being asked questions for which you have no answers and being tortured for your refusal to comply."

"How did I end up here?" Corbin asked the stranger. "When I fell asleep, it was as if Klein pulled me back into this place! How did he do that?"

"Klein has found a way to bind our minds to this place," the stranger said. "You have two bodies now. One lives in Wakeworld, and the other lives here, in the Winterland. When one body sleeps, the other body wakes. When one body wakes, the other body sleeps."

Corbin took a moment to reflect on this statement, unsure whether he should believe it or not. Surely this had to be a dream, he told himself; unpleasant though it was, it was not as if it he was actually there, in the flesh.

"How do I get out of here?" he asked.

"The cell that you are in used to be mine," the voice croaked. "I escaped from it several times before Klein wised up and moved all of us into different cells."

"How?" Corbin asked. "How did you get out of this cell?"

There was another bout of coughing, and then the answer came to him as a feeble whisper:

"It doesn't matter."

"Don't you go quiet on me!" Corbin cried and frantically rattled the bars in the door, drawing distant shrieks and clucking sounds from somewhere down the hallway on his left.

"Please," Corbin implored again, more quietly this time. "Tell me how to escape this cell…. You son of a bitch, *how do I get out of here?!*"

Chains rattled as the form in the opposite cell lunged forward into the light. The man was pale, skinny, and naked, and the black hair on his head and chin was so thin that the skin showed through underneath. He was bound to the floor by three chains attached to rings that pierced his wrists and his jawbone. The skin across his forehead, his eyelids, and the bridge of his long, crooked nose had been peeled off and replaced by a solid strip of slightly darker skin, leaving the faintest trace of a scar and rendering him disfigured and blind.

"Why the fuck would you *want* to get out of here?!" the man demanded. "Why would you want to bring Klein's wrath down upon yourself? Even if you got out of that cell, what then? Do you really imagine that you could get past those monsters and escape this castle? Say you could. What then? How long do you think you would survive out there, in the Winterland?!"

Corbin stared at the man's mutilated face, repulsed and sickened by the evidence of the simple yet ghastly surgery it had been subjected to. At last, he managed to reply:

"I found my way into this nightmare. If you'll only help me to escape from this cell, then I'm sure that I can find my way out of it again."

The man groaned and shook his head, rattling the chain that hung from his jaw.

"I once felt as you do. I was mistaken. *You* are mistaken. You will be caught, and your situation will be that much more dismal for it. The doorway through which you came into the Winterland will not allow you to pass through it again. You want to know how I escaped from that cell? Fine. I will tell you. But don't blame me when Klein or his monsters find you and you realize that you've only made things that much worse for yourself."

"Fair enough," Corbin agreed. "Tell me."

"If you feel above the frame of the door," the man said, "you will find a key. I made it. I shattered my own leg, chewed it off at the knee, and stripped away the flesh. I carved the key out of a splinter of bone, using bits of stone that I found on the floor."

Corbin stood up on his tiptoes and felt along the ledge over the door. Near the center, his fingers brushed a six-inch-long shaft. Upon recovering it, he saw that the item was, in truth, a key, befouled by clots of blood and other unrecognizable filth that had become slick with moisture from the walls. It did, in fact, appear to have been carved out of bone.

"If you made the key out of your own leg bone," Corbin inquired, "how come you still have both of your legs?"

The man hummed thoughtfully for a moment, and then he offered:

"I've always had an exceptionally healthy immune system."

At this, the man burst into a fit of maniacal laughter. Corbin regarded the slimy key with a measure of disdain, wondering just whose body the bone had actually come from.

"The key took me three days to make," the man went on, fighting to keep his mirth in check. "Over the course of those days, occasions arose during which I was forced to hide the key. I had to put it somewhere safe; somewhere where Klein and his monsters would never find it. I kept it in the safest place that I could think of…. I concealed it deep within my rectum."

Corbin let out a soft exclamation of disgust, the nature of the filth which coated the key finally becoming clear to him. He reflexively let it fall from his fingers, and the blind man burst into laughter once more.

"You're squeamish!" the man howled. "You're squeamish about getting another man's shit on your fingers! I bet you're one of those boys who folds the toilet paper before wiping your ass, ain't ya? Too timid to wipe with a single ply of paper, but sure as hell brave enough to go running out into the Winterland. You won't last a day out there! Not an hour!"

His laughter turned into a fit of coughing, and a spray of blood and maggots erupted from his lungs and splattered on the floor. The man fell onto his hands and knees and started licking the floor, eagerly lapping and slurping up blood and maggots with the feverish trembling of a man on the verge of starvation. Corbin, nearly gagging at the sight, bent down and recovered the key with a shaking hand.

"After the key was finished," the man told him between greedy slurps, "I escaped three times. The first time, Klein's monsters found me not twenty feet from here. The second time, Klein himself found me, lost, wandering through the labyrinth of stairways and halls. The third and last time I was captured, I had made it out of the castle and back to the passageway through which I had first entered the Winterland. It was all for nothing. The doorway was shut to me."

"I'll take my chances," Corbin said, reaching through the bars and inserting the key into the lock. The rusty bolt turned, and then the door swung inward with a squeal of metal on metal.

Corbin ventured out into the hallway and looked both ways. The hall ran well over a hundred feet to the right before it turned, and it ran to the left as far as he could see. There were rows of barred doors running down either side for the entire length of the hall. There were torches mounted between every third door, set in metal brackets that were fastened to the walls. Corbin crossed the hall and began attempting to insert the key into the blind man's cell door.

"What are you doing?!" the man cried.

"We're getting out of here," Corbin said, though even as the words left his lips, he realized that it was impossible. The key did not fit in the blind man's lock.

"*Leave me!*" the man howled, shrinking back from the door. "For God's sake, leave me! I've suffered enough! Never again! Oh, please, God! Never again!"

Corbin watched in a combined state of disgust and pity as the man rocked back and forth, cradling his head in his hands and weeping.

"The key won't work in your door," Corbin replied sullenly.

"Oh, thank God!" the man sobbed. "I don't want to escape. I have no further illusions of hope. I only want Klein to leave me alone! I only want him to forget about me. Everybody else has. My friends; my family; my sister…. Oh, God! My sweet sister! They've all forgotten about me."

The blind man's gaunt form was shaken by another fit of coughing. Corbin continued to stand at the door, overcome by sympathy for the man's pain and grief.

"I am so sorry," he said, being unable to find any more adequate words to convey how deeply moved he was.

"I don't want your pity," the man moaned after his coughing had subsided. "Please, just go. And put the key back where you found it. You may need to use it again."

Corbin crossed the hallway once more, checking both ways for anything that might have been drawn by the sound of the blind man's cries. He returned the key to the top of the doorframe and reentered the hallway.

"I don't suppose you could tell me which way to go from here?" Corbin whispered. "You said you made it out of the castle once. Do you remember the way?"

The blind man did not acknowledge him. He merely continued to rock back and forth, cradling his head, his sobs periodically interrupted by heavy rasps and coughs.

Corbin cocked his head and listened. He was fairly certain that he was picking up on the echo of one of Klein's minions clucking in the distance, but he could not be sure whether it was coming from his left or his right. He recalled that Klein had gone to the right, while the second minion had come from and subsequently retreated to the left. While he was more terrified of the prospect of running into Klein, he knew that the yellow-skinned creature had been close by more recently, so he began to walk with soft steps and an attentive ear down the hallway to his right.

As he was passing by the next pair of cells, a voice on his right hissed:

"*Hey!*"

A stocky teenage boy was gripping the bars in the door of his cell and staring at Corbin, his blue eyes wide with fear. He had buzzed blond hair and was wearing a white undershirt and blue boxers. The boy smiled hopefully, revealing a blackened and rotten left canine tooth. Behind him, Corbin saw a hanging birdcage much like the one in his own cell. Inside it was another wicker bird doll built around a reddish-brown globe with a ghostly, hand-like clump trapped within.

"So," the teenager whispered, "the key worked?"

Corbin heard the sound of footsteps behind him and turned around. A tall, naked woman of about thirty with long black hair came stumbling toward him and fell onto her knees. Her brown eyes were bloodshot from weeping, she had a faded scar between her breasts, and she was wearing a leather mask that covered her face from her chin to just below her nose. The mask had a large, toothy grin drawn across it in red and white paint that stood in almost comical contrast to the silent pleading in her eyes.

"Hey!" the teenage boy hissed desperately, regaining Corbin's attention. "I take it the key didn't work in the door across from you, huh? Do you think there's any chance that it might work on this one?"

Corbin stammered uneasily, and his eyes returned almost involuntarily to the woman in the opposite cell. Realizing that she had regained his attention, the woman reached behind her head and undid the leather strap that held the painted mask in place. When she removed it, Corbin saw that the woman had no mouth. It was as if the skin had been peeled off of the lower half of her face and replaced with a solid flap of skin which had merged almost seamlessly with the rest of her face, rendering her mute. The woman cocked her head and regarded him in a questioning manner, almost as if she were waiting for him to tell her how she looked.

"*Hey!*" the teenager repeated, snapping his fingers at Corbin several times in rapid succession. The gesture reminded Corbin of somebody calling a dog to heel, and felt a burning resentment welling up inside him. "Eyes on me, kid! How about you go back to your cell, grab that key, and see if you can't get me and my mates out of here?!"

Corbin did not answer. He was fairly certain that the key would not work on any lock other than his own, and in any case, he had to keep moving. It was not as if he were actually leaving anybody behind, he told himself; he was having a nightmare, and this teenager was nothing but a treacherous part of his own subconscious attempting to slow him down. Without a word, he resumed his journey down the hallway.

"Are you serious?!" the teenage boy exclaimed. "Really?... Come on, dude! You can't just leave us here!"

Corbin ignored him. Behind the next door on his left, he saw a thin, mangled man standing with his back turned toward him beneath a wicker bird constructed about a milky white globe. The man looked as if he had been burned, his skin having grown back as an irregular mass of discolored tissue. His legs were long, skinny, and birdlike, and his body was listing awkwardly to one side.

At the sound of Corbin's approach, the man turned, revealing that his skin had regrown over his crossed arms in such a manner that it had fused both limbs and his chest into a single lump of cratered tissue. He had neither ears, nose, nor genitals, his mouth was sealed shut, and his eyes were white. The man began to rush toward Corbin, his body tottering unsteadily as his feet padded gingerly upon the floor. Once he reached the door, he began to throw himself against it and to bounce off of the bars, making muffled hooting sounds that seemed to originate from deep within his sinus cavity.

Corbin tore his eyes away from the nightmarish image and glanced into the cell on his right. An obese boy with curly black hair who looked as if he were still in middle school was pressed against the bars. He was wearing white briefs, had large lips that gave his face an eternally pouty look, and had snot running from his nose. Corbin saw that the boy had a fresh wound in his chest similar to the one in his own, and behind him there was a wicker bird with a brown ball at the center.

"*Please,*" the boy sobbed as Corbin walked away from him.

In the next cell on his left, Corbin saw a balding man hanging from the ceiling by two lengths of chain. The chains ended in copper rings that appeared to loop around the man's collarbones, though it was hard to tell for sure, because his body had been stitched up in a tight leather sack that encased him from his feet to just over his upper lip. The man was hanging over a stone firepit full of glowing coals. The sack was steaming from the heat and wriggling with the man's efforts to escape, and there was a look of unspeakable agony in his red, smoke-blurred eyes.

Realizing that the most horrific spectacles so far had all been housed in the cells on his left, Corbin decided that he was not going to look in that direction anymore. He ventured a wary glance into the cell on his right, and there was a boy of about twelve clad in red pajamas standing beneath a blue globe. The boy shook his head disapprovingly and declared:

"You really won't get far without our help."

The next cell contained a dark-haired girl in a white T-shirt and gray shorts. The sphere inside her wicker bird was of a deep reddish coloration, and the girl herself was seated so far back in the shadows that Corbin could only just make out the shape of her crossed arms and bowed head. In the next cell was a young, skinny teenage girl with blonde hair that looked almost white in the dim lighting. She was wearing a white crop top and gray sweatpants and was furiously pacing behind the door of her cell. There was a wicker bird with a purplish globe at its core hanging behind her.

"I hope they get you," the girl hissed at Corbin as he passed. "I hope they rip you open and leave you to bleed out!"

The next cell contained a boy in his early teens. The boy was wearing white, waterlogged pajamas and was sitting beneath a birdcage. Inside the cage was a doll built around a lime green globe.

"You got some gall," the boy grunted, "leaving the rest of us here to rot."

Corbin kept walking, and the next cell on his right sent a shudder through him. Kneeling on the floor with outstretched arms beneath a wicker bird built around a cloudy, bluish-white sphere was a woman of about thirty-five. Her pale, bare skin and dark hair were soaked in blood. She was held fast in a statuesque pose by over a hundred strands of barbed wire that came off of metal rings fastened to the floor, walls, and ceiling. The wire twisted all around and throughout her flesh, weaving between ribs, piercing through limbs and pulling her jaw downward so that she appeared to be releasing a silent, never-ending scream.

Prior to this discovery, Corbin had thought that the cells on the right side of the hallway were all reserved for newer, fresher victims such as himself, while the older and more disfigured prisoners were kept on the left. This latest sight disillusioned him, and he resolved to proceed with his eyes fixed upon the ground from then on.

He continued his long march down the cold hallway, choking on an ever-increasing stench of rot, feces, and blood.

Every step he took was accompanied by the sound of rattling chains, muffled cries, and delirious moans. His stomach began to heave in a manner which reminded him of a time when he had been eight years old and had eaten an entire bag of Swedish Fish, and he half-imagined that he could smell the aroma of lingonberries mingled with the stench of urine, feces, and infection that permeated the hall.

It seemed as if an eternity had passed by the time he reached the point where the hallway made a ninety-degree turn to the left. He took the turn, and before long, he came to a point where he had a choice of either going straight or turning left once more. It was at this juncture that he found himself facing an old man hanging on a wall.

The man looked as if he had to have been close to ninety years old. He bore a faded white scar in the middle of his chest, and he had long gray hair and a beard that reached down to his navel. His skin appeared to have been peeled off of his back, his buttocks, and his arms, opened up like an umbrella, and pressed and woven into a metal grate that had been built into the wall behind him. It seemed as if his skin had continued to spread outward after this operation, sending out fingers of growth that had snaked throughout the grating like vines. Hanging from the ceiling above the old man was yet another birdcage. The fleshy ropes from which the wicker bird inside had been crafted had become as dry as leather. The doll was slumped over and unmoving, and the globe around which it had been constructed was milky and white.

The old man lifted his head and blinked a few times, regarding Corbin with an air of disappointment.

"You won't get far," he murmured.

No sooner had he said this than Corbin heard a clucking sound coming from farther down the hall. He saw one of the yellow-skinned creatures squatting about fifty feet away, sitting on its haunches and sniffing at the air.

Corbin looked down the hallway on his left. At its end, a little over thirty feet away, was a large open window. Corbin ran toward it, past the hanging man, and the creature let out a shriek.

The window seemed impossibly far away and his legs were beginning to quiver with exhaustion. When he glanced backward, he saw that the creature was less than twenty feet away, closing the distance at an alarming rate, and that two more monsters had appeared behind it. Corbin ran on, the sounds of his pursuers getting closer and closer, until they sounded so close that he expected to feel one of them pounce upon his back at any moment. He reached the window in a bounding leap, one foot briefly making contact with the stone ledge as he hurdled himself through it, and then he was soaring through open space.

Corbin was plummeting through empty darkness. He saw a moat full of dark water with sleek black stones protruding from its surface a full five stories below him. Icy wind cut through his pajamas and stung his eyes as he plummeted toward the watery abyss, and then he smacked its surface. The force of the impact hammered the air out of his chest while simultaneously forcing water down his throat, and then he struck a submerged rock with a muffled cracking sound. His ribcage shattered, and he felt something tugging him backward, and then he woke up in his own bed, dry and safe.

He sat up and drew a sharp breath. He perched himself on the edge of the bed, struggling to shake off the lingering feeling of panic. He was not being chased, he reminded himself; he was not drowning, and his bones were not broken. He was safe. He was home. Whether it had been a nightmare, or some fantastical out-of-body experience, he had escaped, and a warm sensation of relief began to wash over him. After a few minutes, Corbin lay back down with a contented sigh.

I got out, he thought as he allowed his eyes to drift shut. *Whatever that was—a dream, or a literal second body made as a prison for my mind—I killed it. It's dead, and I'm out, and I'm never going anywhere near that basement again.*

In less than half an hour, Corbin went back to sleep. At that exact moment, he felt himself being yanked out of his warm bed. The next thing he knew, he was lying on his back on the floor of his cell in the Winterland, gazing up at the metal birdcage. He sat up, and when he did so, he saw that Klein was standing in front of him with his sickle in his hand.

"But," Corbin whispered in confusion and horror, "I got out!"

"No," Klein assured him. "You were only dreaming."

Klein swung his arm, and the sickle's blade swiped across Corbin's stomach. The first thing that Corbin felt was a sensation similar to being punched, and that sensation was immediately followed by a sting of pain deep inside him and the feeling of something like a coil of wet rope spilling onto his lap. At that instant, the alarm in his parents' room went off, mercifully waking him.

Chapter Ten
Beyond Help and Hope

Corbin did not go downstairs to have breakfast with his father that morning. He simply lay in bed, gazing up at the ceiling until the sun was shining brightly over the top of his window air conditioning unit.

He dreaded the thought of getting out of bed and living through another day, but he was more afraid of going back to sleep. He wondered if he was going to dream about being back in that cell every night for the rest of his life. Maybe, he tried to tell himself, the dreams were nothing more than a chain reaction; perhaps each dream took such a toll on his mind that it inspired yet another dream, and maybe, he reasoned further, if he could bury them deep enough under more positive thoughts, they would end.

They had a trip to the lake coming up. Until then, he could go out and ride his bike. Would that be enough? He wanted to believe that it would, but a dark, unravelling corner of his mind refused to let go of the notion that he had nothing to look forward to but endless nights of suffering and, eventually, death.

He wondered how late in the day it was. Had Dominic, Thomas, and Angela already left without him? Had they even bothered to come looking for him after he had failed to show up on the previous morning? He had not heard them yet, but he thought it must have been after seven. It broke his heart a little to think that they might have given up on him, but the thought also provided a measure of comfort. Corbin knew that he could never hope to make his friends understand the emptiness that was eating away at him. There were no words to explain the fleeting ideas and fragments of dialogue that were racing though his head, coming together and disintegrating in an endless stream of disconnected gibberish. Corbin could never explain these things, nor did he feel that he deserved the chance to try.

Broken. Out of the midst of the chaotic flow of thoughts racing through his mind, this one word lingered a half a beat longer than the rest, like a tree branch that drags across the shoreline whilst being swept away on a flooded, driftwood-choked river. *Broken. You are a …*

"… Broken thing." The words escaped his mouth, shattering the stillness of the morning. He sat up violently, his heart starting to race with panic. Had his mother heard him? Would she come upstairs to find out what was wrong? Would she realize that he had lost his mind and have him locked away somewhere? Somewhere where he could not hurt himself, and where the doctors would keep him alive so that he could go on dreaming about the Winterland night after night?

You need to calm down. He forced the words to the forefront of his mind, pushing back against the chaotic tide of endless noise. *You need to calm down…. You need to calm down.*

He allowed the phrase to play in his mind, over and over, keeping rhythm with the thrumming of the air conditioner until its mechanical groanings seemed to recite the words back to him. Before long, he stopped reciting the mantra, but the air conditioner refused to give up the chant, and the words started to take on a harsh, scolding tone:

YOU NEED TO CALM DOWN!… YOU NEED TO CALM DOWN!

Corbin winced and covered his ears. The words had become so loud that he could not imagine his mother failing to hear them, and he could think of no easy way to explain to her why his air conditioner was screaming at him.

"No," he hissed, casting a hateful glare in the direction of the air conditioner, "*you* need to…."

He stopped himself, realizing that he was speaking to a lifeless piece of equipment. The air conditioner was no longer shouting anything intelligible, and Corbin supposed that it never had been. Air conditioners were, after all, incapable of speech.

Air conditioners aren't incapable of speech in dreams, he reminded himself. *If your air conditioner says anything else, then you'll know that you are dreaming.*

The air conditioner had nothing to say to that. Either it was on to him, or it was, in fact, nothing more than an air conditioner. In any case, Corbin decided that it would be best to turn it off. The realization that the Georgia heat would soon turn his room into a virtual oven did not trouble him. He did not feel much anymore anyway, and warmth least of all.

As he stepped out into the hall and approached the stairway, it occurred to him that his legs were moving a fraction of a second later than he was willing them to. Feeling unbalanced, he began to drag his right shoulder across the wall to steady himself. Furthermore, he did not like the way that the shadows seemed to play across the edge of his peripheral vision, and he was starting to become convinced once more that there was something amiss— some undeniable evidence that this version of reality was flawed— hiding just out of sight.

Corbin entered the dining room. His mother was in the kitchen, washing dishes that he assumed were left over from his father's breakfast. She looked over her shoulder at the sound of his footsteps and gave him a bright smile.

"Good morning!" she gushed cheerfully. "Managed to catch up on some sleep, did you?"

Corbin sighed wearily.

"Yeah," he replied sourly. "I slept a lot better than I have been."

He did not consider this to be a lie. He had, in truth, spent more time asleep than on the previous night. The fact that he had not been asleep nearly as long as she thought, or that he did not feel the least bit rested, seemed irrelevant, considering how the question had been worded.

"No more dreams?" she asked, returning her attention to the dishes in the sink. The gurgling and splashing of water cascading from the faucet made Corbin feel nauseous, and he collapsed weakly into a chair at the dining room table.

"Nothing like the dreams I've been having," he answered.

Again, it was not exactly a lie.

"Glad to hear it!" she said, and her obliviously cheerful tone irritated Corbin. He knew that it was unfair of him to be angry with his mother, considering that he had misled her into thinking that he was doing better, but he held onto the feeling nonetheless. He had been empty for far too long, and this newfound feeling of anger filled him up like a warm bowl of soup.

"You want two eggs or three?" she asked.

"Two's fine," Corbin grunted.

"Sausages as well?"

Corbin clenched his teeth and sharply drew in breath, trying to keep his temper in check.

Dear God! Does she ever stop talking?

"No, thank you. I'm not all that hungry."

"You want some apple juice? Or orange, or grape?"

Corbin wondered if his father ever thought about cutting out his mother's tongue to get her to shut up, and he found himself briefly imagining the sound of a serrated blade clinking and scraping against her teeth. This unwelcome thought departed as quickly as it had come, leaving him feeling ashamed.

"Apple juice would be good. Thank you."

Corbin could not bear the thought of staying inside with his mother all day, trying to say all the things that a normal person might say. He had to get away from her, from the house, and from his own troubled thoughts.

"I think," he ventured, "I'm feeling well enough to go for a bike ride, later, after breakfast."

Emily turned away from the sink once more, this time regarding him with a studious gaze.

"You sure you're up for that?" she asked.

Corbin nodded eagerly.

"Oh, sure!" he said. "I think some exercise, sunshine, and hanging out with friends would do me a lot of good."

The bikers had ridden on without him, but Corbin thought he could safely guess where they had gone: to the waterfall off of Hemlock Drive.

Emily seemed to weigh the idea in her mind for a minute, and then she smiled.

"Yeah, it probably would," she said. "I'm glad you're feeling up to it!"

Little more was said between then and the time Corbin finished his breakfast, at which point he retreated into the basement and recovered his bike. His legs felt clumsy, and the bike's front tire kept turning sideways and catching on the steps as he forced the machine up the stairway that led to their backyard. By the time he had made his way to the street, Corbin felt tired in a way that went beyond mental or physical exhaustion. It was as if the tired had seeped into his bones, and he briefly considered dropping the bike where it stood and heading back into the house. There was nothing for him in the house, however, but endless hours of misery. At least out there, on the road, the misery would be of a less familiar nature, so he mounted his bike and began to slowly pedal away to the west.

There was a haze of humidity laying over Devland like a weighted blanket, trapping and compounding the summer heat. Sweat was stinging Corbin's eyes and soaking through his shirt by the time he made it to Margo Street and turned east toward Clair's. He made it as far as the Picture Palace, at which point he made a left and headed north through a narrow alley. Soon he turned back east onto a gravel lane called Aucuba Way, but before long, he felt compelled to head farther north, down a well-paved and shaded road that seemed to be taking him toward the edge of the Devland township.

Corbin realized that he was procrastinating, and he suddenly understood that, contrary to what he had told his mother, he had no actual desire to meet up with his friends that day. All he wanted to do was ride, feel the wind on his face, and allow the repetitive activity of pedaling his bike to drown out his thoughts. He was not going to make it as far as the waterfall, and that was okay. He might make it far as Clair's, though he was not sure; as hot as he was, it would have been nice to get something to drink, but he did not relish the prospect of having to interact with people to get one. If he did not, however, he imagined that he might die of thirst. He decided that would be okay too.

Why, he pondered bitterly, had he been stupid enough to wander into that nightmare again? That puzzle box had just seemed too important, too enticing, for him to leave it alone. He felt a burning resentment toward Angela for having urged him to try to open the damn thing. He knew that it was not her fault—not really—but he hated her for it nonetheless.

This is your dream!

He could almost hear her voice, thinly masked beneath the whirring of his bike's spokes:

You have to look inside the box…. It may well have been the most important part of the dream!

Then, another voice—the voice of the Frog Catcher—came to mind:

Soon, you may never be able to wake up again, no matter how much fear is in your heart nor how much pain is in your flesh.

Corbin ran his bike into a ditch full of damp leaves and brought it to a hurried stop, wanting to cry, wanting to scream, but unable to produce so much as a sob. He sat astride his bike, sweat pouring down his face and breathing heavily, allowing the wet summer heat to press upon him and wishing he had not lived to see such miserable days.

That evening, as he sat down to a dinner of pot roast and mashed potatoes, he found his parents in an uncharacteristically cheerful mood. It made sense, he supposed: He had slept in. He had gone to great efforts to convince his mother that he was feeling better. So far as they knew, things were finally starting to look up.

If they only knew....

"So, Corbin," James said between mouthfuls of roast, "I missed you at breakfast this morning! No more dreams about underground forests?"

"Nope," Corbin said, nudging a fatty shred of meat in tight circles across his plate. "No forests."

"I'm glad to hear it," James went on, oblivious to the wretchedness in his tone. "Your mother said you went out riding with your friends again. Did you have a good time?"

"It did me a world of good!" Corbin declared with a hearty nod. He felt awful, but he was certain that he felt better than he would have if he had not bothered to go. He saw no need to correct his father about the fact that he had never actually met up with the other bikers.

Dreading the possibility of an early bedtime that night, he added:

"Actually, I feel well enough that I was hoping we might stay up and watch a movie tonight."

Emily frowned slightly.

"Shouldn't you be focusing on catching up on a bit more sleep tonight?" she asked. "You still look a bit run-down."

Corbin had anticipated this objection, and he had his rebuttal prepared:

"Tomorrow's Saturday! We can sleep in as late as we want tomorrow."

James laughed.

"Just because it's the weekend doesn't mean that the fun stops!" he pointed out. "Don't forget, we're going to visit the lake tomorrow. Then, on Sunday, we have Uncle Kurt's cookout to look forward to!"

Corbin's heart sank. The lake had slipped his mind, and he had completely forgotten about the cookout.

"But, yeah," James said, "it would be nice to watch something."

"Any word on when we might get cable?" Emily asked.

James sighed.

"Yeah," he groaned, "I keep meaning to look into that on my lunchbreak. I never can seem to remember. Do you suppose that's something that you would want to look into?"

"Sure, I'll take care of it. Corbin, did you have something specific that you wanted to watch tonight?"

"*The Lord of the Rings,*" Corbin blurted out without hesitation.

That'll make bedtime come a bit later, all right.

After dinner, the three of them sat through the extended edition of *The Fellowship of the Ring* before brushing their teeth and making their way to bed at a little past eleven. Corbin's room was stiflingly hot, so he turned on his window air conditioning unit before he lay down. For about forty-five minutes, Corbin lay on his back and stared at the ceiling, feeling hot and uncomfortable and dreading what might be waiting for him on the other side of sleep. He had put off bedtime for as long as he could. He had tried his best not to dwell on his previous dreams and to chase all memory of them from his head. He wondered: would it be enough to break the cycle?

At length, he rolled over onto his side and allowed his mind to rest. It took him close to half an hour more to fall asleep, at which point he woke with a jolt on the stone floor of his cell.

"No," he groaned. "Please, God! *No!*"

He started to sit up, and as he did so, he felt a stab of pain deep in his gut. He perceived that he was sitting in the middle of a pool of blood. Turning his eyes downward, he let out a scream of horror at the sight of the wet, sticky pile of intestines that had spilled out of his belly.

Chapter Eleven
Dolls and Other Playthings

Corbin was afraid to move, but he was still more afraid to remain where he was and continue to bleed out. He held his trembling hands over the steaming pile of blood-smeared entrails, feeling the heat radiating off of them, wanting to try to push them back inside himself but loathing to touch them. His frantic, gasping breaths started to turn into shuddering sobs, and thence into outright wails of horror, pain, and despair.

He heard the sound of laughter coming from the cell across from him, quickly replaced by a wet, hacking cough.

"*Please!*" Corbin begged, though he knew that there was nothing the blind man could do to help him.

"Leave me alone," the blind man groaned.

Corbin sat there for what must have been close to an hour, paralyzed by agony and uncertainty. At last, he delicately scooped up his intestines, cradling them in the crook of his left arm as one might carry a baby, and forced himself first to his knees and then to his feet. He walked, doubled over with pain, across his cell to the barred door.

He forced his body to stand erect and reached for the key, and as he did so, a stab of pain nearly brought him to his knees. A fold of his intestines began to slip off of his arm and he doubled over again, fearful that he might drop them and send the remainder of his insides pouring out of him like yarn being pulled out of the center of a skein. After he had regained control of the slippery bundle, which was by then beginning to rupture and to ooze fresh blood and feces, he rose up to full height again and closed his fingers around the key on top of the ledge.

Corbin slumped back down and inserted the key into the lock, not bothering to listen for the clucks and chitters of Klein's minions.

"What are you doing?!" the blind man cried.

"I'm getting out of here," Corbin replied weakly as he swung the door open. Then he rose up to his full heigh once more and slipped the key back onto the ledge.

"Ah, you found the key," the blind man whispered. "I remember the key. I made it out of a bone from my own leg. I shattered my knee, chewed through the flesh, and carved it using bits of stone."

Corbin stared into the shadow in which the blind man lay.

"Do you remember me?" he asked.

"When you've finished," the blind man went on, ignoring the question, "be sure to put the key back where you found it. You may need it again. Then, go and leave me alone. Forget about me. Everybody else has. Everybody has...."

The blind man's words trailed off into a stream of unintelligible mutterings interspersed with wheezing breaths. Corbin eased the door shut behind him and started to walk down the hall to his right.

Each step he took required a Herculean effort, and after a few paces, he fell to his knees. His intestines flopped onto the floor with a wet slap, the weight of their fall tearing them even farther out of Corbin's body. His muscles clenched and he started to shake, and at length he simply lay down, curled up around the steaming heap, and wept.

"Last night didn't work out quite the way you wanted it to, huh?"

Corbin opened his eyes. He saw the teenage boy in the white undershirt grasping the bars of his cell door and staring at him. The teenager grimaced, his rotten canine glistening like wet silver in the flickering torchlight.

"*Guys!*" the teenager hissed. "It's that boy from last night! Klein tore him up but good."

Corbin heard the pattering of feet and a slight rattling sound as the other prisoners clutched and pressed against the bars of their cells, eager to catch a glimpse of him, and he heard the sound of a girl's laughter. He started to rub the tears out of his eyes, smearing blood across his face as he did so, and whispered:

"I didn't pay any attention to you last night."

In the distance, he heard the boy in the white pajamas reply:

"Huh! Yeah, that about sums it up, all right."

"You seem pretty anxious to talk now, though," the teen in the undershirt observed, "now that you need our help."

"I didn't pay attention," Corbin attempted to explain, "because I didn't think you were *real*. I thought you were all just a part of my dream."

The teen in the undershirt scowled at Corbin coldly.

"I am the most real person you're going to find in this hellish farce," he said. "And as for this being *your* dream…. Well, if I thought there was even a chance of that, I'd reach through these bars and wring that scrawny neck of yours."

"Last night," Corbin raised his voice, addressing the boy in the red pajamas, "you said that I wouldn't get far without your help."

The teen in the undershirt snorted.

"Looks like Zack got that one right," he muttered humorlessly.

"What did you mean by that?" Corbin shouted down the hallway. "How does one get out of this place?"

"Before we start getting into all of that," the teen in the undershirt said, loudly enough for the boy down the hall to hear him, "how about you go and get that key of yours? See if it doesn't work in one or more of these other doors?"

"The key only fits in my lock," Corbin assured him. "I already tried it in the door across from mine."

"Well, why don't you try it in *this* door and just see what happens?" the teen countered. "Just for shits and giggles."

"Perhaps there are other keys around," the obese boy in the white briefs added hopefully.

"There is only *one key!*" Corbin cried without regard for who or what might hear him, overcome by misery and frustration. "It was made to fit the lock in *my door!* Do I look like I'm in any state to go out looking for other keys, or to go back and forth trying things that I already know won't work?! Last night, you implied that you knew of a way out. Are you going to help me or not?!"

A moment of silence prevailed. At last, he heard the girl with the blonde hair reply:

"After the way you treated us last night, why would we want to help you?"

"Yeah," the teen in the undershirt said, beginning to withdraw from the door. "If you're not gonna do the same for us, what's the point? Why don't you just crawl back into that cell of yours and try to stuff all that shit back inside you. Either way, please, go away. You're making a bloody mess, and your guts stink."

Corbin continued to lie on the cold stone floor, wracked by pain and devoid of hope. Finally, he said:

"Just tell me how to get out of here, and I promise I will come back for you."

The teen in the undershirt regarded him cynically.

"Even if you found a way to open our cell doors, why would we believe that you'd come back?"

"Because you don't have a choice," Corbin said. "Maybe I won't make it back. Maybe I won't even make it out of this hallway. But it's a chance, and that's more than you've got right now."

The teen in the undershirt stared at Corbin, a mixture of vexation and disgust on his face. Then, the voice of the boy in the red pajamas came floating down the hall:

"We don't know the way out of this place. What we do know is that those yellow-skinned creatures—the malignants, Klein calls them—are blind. They use sonar to navigate these halls, like bats. That's why you always hear them clucking before you see them. Keep your ears open, and if you hear a malignant headed your way, get yourself flat against a wall. Blend yourself in with the rocks, and they should walk right past you."

The teen in the undershirt let out a disgruntled huff, seemingly annoyed that the boy in the red pajamas had taken control of the situation away from him.

"I will come back for you," Corbin repeated his promise.

"Yeah, sure," the teen muttered. "Thanks. I'm feeling much better already."

Corbin began to crawl away, dragging himself across the stones with his left forearm and right leg, using his right arm to cradle and guide his intestines. Slowly, painfully, he slid himself past the cell that held the fat boy in the white briefs, and then the one that housed the boy in the red pajamas. Corbin could feel the skin on his left hip becoming raw, and his intestines were rapidly degrading into a gored, formless mass of ruptured and bloody tissue. He forced his way past the cells of the girl wearing the white T-shirt and gray shorts, the girl in the white crop top and sweatpants, and the boy in the white pajamas, and yet, in spite of the distance he had come, the end of the hall still seemed so very, very far away.

For what seemed like ages, Corbin crawled. These ages were made up of countless repetitive motions: gathering up his intestines with his fingers; cradling them in the crook of his arm; raising up his torso with his left elbow; pulling his body forward; pushing himself along with right foot. Then again, and again, as mindless and as eternal as the earth making laps around the sun, until he finally found himself gazing upon the old, half-skinned man attached to the wall.

The old man lifted his bearded chin from his breast, opened his eyes, and regarded Corbin with an expression of pity.

"You still won't get far," the man said.

Corbin rolled onto his back, physically and mentally spent.

"You said that last night," Corbin groaned. "I made it out, but then I found myself right back in my cell. Is that how it works? We escape, but then we wake up right back where we started?"

"If you want to get out of here," the hanging man said, "first, you must go back to that window that you ran to last night, and you must jump."

Corbin scoffed, the sound coming out as a syrupy gurgle in the back of his throat.

"Already tried that."

"The jump is almost certain to kill you," the hanging man continued, "but I suggest that you aim for one of the rocks below and make sure of it."

"All that's gonna do is wake me up," Corbin argued. "The next time I fall asleep, I'm just going to end up right back in that cell!"

"You are wounded," the hanging man reminded him calmly. "You are in no fit state to go wandering through the halls of Klein's fortress. Go to the window. Jump, die, and wake up. When you have fallen asleep again, you will find that all of your wounds are healed. Except for the one in your chest, of course; rebirth will neither heal it, nor reopen it once it has healed on its own. Come to me when next you sleep, if you can, and I will tell you how to unbind yourself from that cell."

Corbin stared up at the hanging man uncertainly. The idea made sense—last night, his broken ribs had been mended after he had died, woken up, and gone back to sleep—but, dreaming or not, jumping to his death was not an idea that sat well with him. In the end, however, he knew that he had no real choice in the matter, and he rolled back over onto his side.

"I'll try," he said, and began to crawl away toward the window.

"After you wake up," the hanging man cautioned, "don't dawdle! Your Winterland body will only be reborn when you next fall asleep. If you stay awake for too long and they discover that your cell is empty, they'll be waiting for you. If that should happen, I doubt if Klein would ever give you a chance to come this way again."

Corbin paused for a minute, gathering his strength, and then he began to crawl toward the window with renewed vigor. When he had reached it, he hooked the fingers of his left hand over the sill and pulled himself up onto his knees. Peering over the edge, he saw black, stony waters beneath him and a dark forest beyond. The trees here grew tall and erect under the high ceiling, quite unlike the bent and twisted oaks that had comprised the forest where he had first entered the Winterland. Braziers full of glowing red embers flickered like fiery stars among the distant, shadowy boughs and gleamed upon the wet stones directly below, causing them to glisten like black shards of glass.

He dragged himself up and sat on the sill, hanging his legs over the side and cradling his innards in his lap, trying to find the courage to push himself off of the wall. In spite of his agony, his survival instincts remained as keen as ever, and he sat and stared down at the black water and glistening stones for a long, long while.

Somewhere behind him, Corbin heard the sound of water slowly dripping.

I'll go on the tenth drip, he told himself, and he began to count: *One…. Two…. Three….*

The tenth drip came and went, but his courage did not come with it. In the end, it was the chittering cry of an approaching malignant rather than his own inner-strength that pushed him over the edge. He shoved himself off in a panic, sending his body tumbling out into space.

The wind caught his intestines as he fell, and they began to tear loose from the fatty tissues that held them in place. They trailed away behind him, tattering and fluttering in the wind and winding about him like snakes as he spun through the cold air. He let out a long, anguished cry until the water struck his back, knocking the wind out of him. He felt his skull crack and his neck twist as his head made contact with a submerged stone, and then he was pulled away and found himself lying upon his bed.

Corbin immediately got to his feet and began to pace the floor. In spite of the fact that the room was still quite warm, he found that he was shivering. He recalled the hanging man's warning: if he did not go back to sleep quickly, the malignants would realize that he had gone. Whether it was a dream or not, Corbin had come to accept that the Winterland was governed by certain rules, and the last thing he wanted to do was fall asleep too late and find Klein standing over him with his sickle drawn.

He lay back down and tried to make himself comfortable, but his heart was still pounding in his chest and he was breathing hard. The fact that he so desperately needed to go back to sleep made him all the more anxious, and he began to toss and turn and finally to sob in desperation. Half an hour passed, and he finally accepted that he was not going to fall asleep anytime soon.

Corbin got back out of bed and went downstairs, pacing himself as he went, trying to keep his heart rate down. He went to the kitchen and filled a glass with water from the sink. He drank it slowly, trying to immerse himself in how cool and refreshing it was, trying not to imagine the torments that he might find waiting for him if he stayed awake for too long. After the glass had been emptied, he set it down on the counter and walked back to his room. He lay down on the bed, tossed and turned for about twenty minutes, and then lay still for another fifteen. At last, he felt himself being wrenched back into his nightmare.

Corbin sat up, his eyes sweeping the cell for intruders. He was alone. He inspected himself, looking for any old or new wounds. The cut across his stomach had healed without leaving so much as a scar, but the wound in the middle of his chest remained. He picked himself up, let himself out of his cell, and started walking down the hall.

"*Hey!*" the teenager in the white undershirt hissed at him. "Did you find anything yet?"

"Keep it down," Corbin urged him. "I'm working on it."

A chorus of grumblings and doubtful scoffs followed him down the hall, and he heard the boy in the white pajamas say: "We should sound the alarm on that lying sack of shit." None of them did, however. At one point, as he was nearing the turn at the end of the hall, he heard several shrieks and a number of clicking sounds coming from somewhere behind him. He considered running back to his cell, but the sounds did not persist, so he continued on his way.

It was not long before Corbin had again reached the hanging man. His head was raised and his eyes were open, as if he had been waiting for Corbin the entire time.

"When Klein split your chest open," the old man began as soon as Corbin had drawn near, "he tore out a fragment of your soul. He is using it as a sort of an anchor, binding you to this world. When you first came to this place, you came as little more than a ghost. Now, Klein has turned you into a real, flesh-and-blood resident of the Winterland. You have two bodies now: one in the real world—or 'Wakeworld,' as Klein calls it—and one that remains here, in the Winterland.

"When your natural body—your Wakeworld body—sleeps, the bond between your soul and the fragment that Klein ripped out of your chest pulls you back into the Winterland. When your Wakeworld body awakens, however, your soul is compelled to return to its natural body. Every time your soul does this, your stolen fragment yearns to be reunited with it, and all of its will gazes after it.

"That is the function of the homunculi; those strange, bird-like dolls of flesh, bone, and leather. As your fragment gazes after your soul, your homunculus's eyes gaze right along with it, following it as far as it can, tracing it back a little closer every day to the doorway through which you first entered the Winterland.

"What Klein does not understand—or rather what he refuses to accept—is that there are hundreds of weak points in the barrier between Wakeworld and the Winterland. Most of them are located in or around the Oakland Forest, but not all of them. He is convinced that, somewhere, there must be a single gateway that we are all conspiring to keep hidden from him, but the truth is that flesh-and-blood creatures such as Klein—and now ourselves—cannot physically pass between worlds. In binding us to the Winterland, all he has done is take away our ability to leave this place, and in so doing has doomed us to the same fate which he somehow brought upon himself."

Corbin's throat felt very dry, and he was becoming aware of a constricted feeling in his chest.

"Do you mean," he asked in a faltering voice, "I can't go back the way I came? If I were to get out this castle, and if I were to find the passageway that connects to my basement back home, I wouldn't be able to use it to leave this place?"

"The one thing that all of the weak points in the barrier have in common," the hanging man told him, "is that no material object can pass through them. Now that Klein has tethered you and given you a physical form, there is no going back. You are trapped in this nightmare. Same as me; same as all these other poor souls; same as Klein himself."

"What exactly is Klein?" Corbin wanted to know. "Was he like us once? Someone that dreamed about this place and got stuck in it?"

"I do not know what he is," the hanging man said, "but I doubt if he was ever human. I know that he wants to be. Clearly, he has been to our world at some point. He desires above all else to return to it and to live there as you and I used to, and he is confused and enraged by his inability to do so."

"Do you know what the Winterland is?" Corbin asked. "Is this a dream, or is it an actual place?"

The hanging man sighed and shook his head.

"I don't know what to believe anymore," he admitted. "I used to believe it was a dream, but who can say? And, if it is a dream, who's dream? And why are we a part of it? I pondered these questions for many years, but I never found any answers, and questioning the nature of the Winterland never got me any closer to escaping from it."

"And, there's really no way out?" The words caught in Corbin's throat, and he realized that he was beginning to feel sick to his stomach. "I'm just stuck here for the rest of my life?"

"To say 'the rest of my life' implies that death would offer you an escape," the old man grunted bitterly. "It doesn't. The destruction of your Wakeworld body does not mean the end of your Winterland body. I tried. I took my own life many, many years ago. All the difference it made is that, now, I no longer have a Wakeworld body to wake up into. This body—this torn and tortured vessel that Klein has crafted for me—is all I have left, perhaps for all of eternity.

"Even so, you might still be able to escape. After you jumped through the window and destroyed your Winterland body, it was recreated close to what looked like a glass ball, was it not?"

"Yes," Corbin confirmed. "That piece of me that Klein tore out of my chest was trapped inside it."

"The Spheres of Torment," the hanging man explained gravely, looking upon the milky-white globe encased in the dry, long-dead homunculus that hung in the birdcage before him. "They are what bind us to this world. Every time we die in the Winterland, we are remade within a short distance of our spheres. If you want to get out of the castle, then you must make the jump along with your sphere, so that you might be reborn outside of the castle's walls."

"And then what?" Corbin asked. "If I can retrieve my sphere, get it outside of the castle and destroy it, will I become whole again and be free?"

"The Spheres of Torment are said to be indestructible," the hanging man told him, "but escaping the castle with your sphere is certainly the first step toward escaping the Winterland."

"But the spheres are all locked up in cages," Corbin pointed out. "How is one supposed to retrieve them?"

"There is a key," the hanging man said. "It unlocks all of the birdcages. Klein has entrusted this key to an entity known as the Chatelaine. I can direct you to the chamber where this creature dwells, but I must warn you that she is almost as dangerous as Klein, herself, and she keeps the key on her person at all times.

"To find her, you must continue down this hall," the hanging man went on, gesturing to his left with a nod of his head. "Follow it until it turns to the right. At that point, take the stairs that will be in front of you. Once you reach the next floor down, take the hall directly ahead and follow it until it splits three ways. Turn left there, and soon you will come to another flight of stairs that will take you down six more stories to a corridor. At the end of this corridor, you will find a door. On the other side of this door lies the chamber of the Chatelaine."

"Down the hall," Corbin recited, "down the stairs, straight ahead, to the left, and down six more stories?"

"Correct."

"If I make it all that way without getting caught, how exactly am I supposed to get the key away from her?"

The hanging man laughed.

"If I knew that, I might have tried it myself."

"This creature—this 'Chatelaine'—I don't suppose she would have any other keys on her, would she? I promised to try to get a few of the others out."

"She holds the keys to every door in this castle," the man said, his brow furrowing with disapproval, "but I would advise you to forget about any promises that you might have made. If you get out of here at all, it will be by the skin of your teeth. If you are somehow that fortunate, I would advise you not to push your luck. Find the key, retrieve your sphere, and leave. If you should steal the keys and be caught, I scarcely dare imagine what Klein might do to you."

Corbin considered the hanging man's words for a moment, and then he shook his head.

"I intend to keep my promise," he said, "and I'm going to come back for you as well."

The hanging man laughed bitterly.

"Look at me, boy! Do I look like I am in any condition to travel? Those monsters—those malignants—would be all over us before you peeled me halfway off this wall."

"I could kill you," Corbin suggested. "Then, wouldn't you be reborn in the same condition in which you first came to the Winterland?"

The old man groaned.

"I don't want you to try to save me," he replied sullenly. "I have suffered enough, and I shudder to think what fresh torments would await me if I were to escape this castle and be recaptured.

Don't feel that you owe me anything, boy. I haven't done you any favors. Even if you defeat the Chatelaine—no small undertaking in itself—what would you do then? Where would you go? The malignants are superb trackers. Even if you could survive the nameless horrors of the Winterland—again, no easy task—eventually, they will find you. I have no hope of escaping this nightmare. Since Klein caught me, there is one lesson that I have learned above all others: there is no place in the Winterland for hope."

Corbin frowned.

"You don't really believe that," he said. "If you did, you wouldn't have bothered to tell me where to find the keys."

The hanging man sighed and hung his head.

"Maybe I just hate Klein so much that I couldn't pass up an opportunity to bring grief upon him," he said, "even in so small a matter as sending a little boy to steal his keys. Maybe I'm just an old fool. Either way, I would prefer staying here to risking recapture, or to taking my chances out there in the wilds of the Winterland. If somehow you do succeed, I shall take comfort enough in knowing that one of Klein's prisoners got the best of him. Go on now. Go on and leave me be."

The old man lowered his chin onto his breast and allowed his eyes to drift shut. Corbin started to walk away. He had nearly rounded the corner when he heard the man call out to him once more:

"If, by chance, you do get out of here and find some means of destroying your sphere, do not hesitate to do so! I am sure you have noticed by now that you are not the same little boy that you once were. You have been feeling out of sorts; confused; having difficulty discerning between what is real and what is not. Am I right?"

Corbin felt the hairs on the back of his neck beginning to stand on end, and he turned back toward the man.

"Yes," he said.

"It will only get worse. The longer your soul remains incomplete, the more unstable your mind will become. If your fragment goes dormant, or if that wound in your chest heals, I don't expect even destroying your sphere and escaping from the Winterland would make much difference as far as your sanity is concerned. I have seen Klein take many prisoners over the years, and I have yet to see a fragment that endured longer than two weeks after it was torn out of a soul and locked away in a Sphere of Torment."

Corbin stared at the man, a feeling of nausea worming its way into his stomach.

"In that case," he whispered, as much for his own benefit as for the hanging man's, "I suppose I had better not waste any time."

With those final parting words, Corbin began the long and lonely walk toward the Chatelaine's lair. The dimly lit hallway ran on for over two hundred feet. Corbin was conscious of the sounds of moaning and stirring behind the barred doors on either side of him, yet he dared not look upon the tortured souls that were making the sounds. As he neared the end of the hall, he heard the clicking of a malignant approaching from around the corner, and he violently threw himself against the wall on his right.

He just had time to inch himself closer to one of the cell doors for better concealment before the blind, bat-eared creature came bounding into view. This one was clearly a male, though the parts that distinguished it as such had withered, and it had two white and sunken eyes that were partly obscured by a mop of thin blond hair. It galloped toward Corbin in the same three-limbed fashion that all of the malignants seemed to employ, its jaw hanging listlessly and drool streaming from its lipless mouth. A second malignant, a female, followed close behind it.

Corbin held his breath. He could feel his heart beginning to race as the creatures approached, beating so hard that he feared they could not help but hear it, but they passed by without seeming to notice him. He watched them until they turned the corner to the right, and then his eyes were drawn to the occupant of the cell across from him.

In the cell, there was man whose body was almost completely devoid of hair. His arms were crossed behind his back, bound in place with rusty wire that had lacerated his oozing flesh nearly to the bone, and he wore a metal collar around his neck. There was a chain running from the collar to the ceiling and another running to the floor, holding him at a height where he could neither squat nor stand up straight. He had a gag in his mouth in the shape of a metal ring, and tracks of yellow, crusty drool and mucus ran down his face, neck, and chest, all the way down to his feet. Hundreds of maggots were writhing in the crusty pool on the floor, and many of them were feeding off of what little flesh was left on his ankles.

Corbin pulled himself off of the wall, took a deep, steadying breath and headed toward the stairway at the end of the hall, keeping his eyes firmly planted on the ground as he did so.

The stairway was of a spiral design, lit only by the torches in the levels above and below it. Here more so than in the hallway, Corbin was reminded of how cold the Winterland was, and the stone steps felt particularly icy on the soles of his tender, aching feet. He reached the next level down and found that the torches there were farther apart and that the stench of feces and rotting flesh was nearly overpowering. The bars on the cell doors appeared much older and more rusted than those above, and Corbin's curiosity got the better of him to the point that he ventured a peek into one of the cells on his right.

Within the cell, he saw an old woman with weights chained to her ankles straddling a peaked wooden sawhorse. The edge of the coarse wooden beam had cut halfway through her bruised and broken pelvis, and her toes were quivering with her efforts to support her weight lest the sawhorse should split her further. Her face was contorted into a mask of hopeless agony that Corbin feared would haunt him for days to come.

He turned away from the sight, making the mistake of allowing his eyes to wander as far as the cell across from hers. In that cell, he saw an old man hanging by chains that connected to metal rings that pierced his wrists. His skin had become baggy and full of holes, draped over his bare muscles like an ill-fitting cheese cloth sack. There were six greenish, eel-like creatures working their way between his skin and his flesh, moving out through one hole and into another, pausing now and then to snip at his raw and tattered muscles. Two gray eyes rolled about in the man's drooping bag of a face, and he was moaning and fitfully chattering his teeth.

These sights, along with the stench, overwhelmed Corbin. He bent over and vomited, retching up a bitter cocktail of mucus and acid that burned this throat and made his nose run. He stumbled onward, spitting repeatedly in an attempt to get the vile taste out of his mouth, nearly blinded by tears and gagging on the snot that was streaming down his face.

Eventually, the hallway split off in three different directions, and he took the turn on his left. There were more rusty doors on either side of him, and he heard more rustling sounds and feeble cries. The longer he walked, the more the sounds seemed to blend into a monotonous tumult that almost seemed to be coming from inside his own head, and he feared that if he did not find the way out soon, the noise would drive him mad.

In time, he came to a well-lit, unbarred doorway on his right, and the sight of it filled him with an unaccountable sense of unease. Corbin crept up to the edge of the doorway, keeping his back pressed against the wall as he did so, and then he leaned over and peered inside.

The room was lit by over a hundred small white candles that had been set up on shelves, in cubbies built into the walls, on a wooden table toward the back of the room, and spread out across the floor. Klein was sitting inside a circle of candles with his back turned toward the door. His legs were folded into a lotus position, and he was muttering and fidgeting in a state of agitation. The malignant named Riddle was lying on her stomach on Klein's right, just outside the circle of candles, moaning and chittering at him in evident adoration.

    Corbin pulled himself clear of the doorframe and pressed his back against the wall even harder. Did he dare to pass by the room, even with Klein's back turned? Seeing as the giant had no eyes, he was not certain that the direction he was facing would make any difference. What about Riddle? Would she hear him or pick up his presence on her sonar? He remained frozen in place, listening, scarcely daring to draw a breath.

    His eyes fell upon the cell directly across from the candle-lit room. Inside it he saw a skinny, naked man hanging from the ceiling, his body speckled with dried blood. His eyes had been gouged out, and a length of barbed wire had been fed through his nose and out through his mouth. Both ends of the wire were fastened to the ceiling, suspending the man by his nasal cavity so that his toes were dangling a few inches above the floor. Another length of barbed wire had been wrapped tightly around the man's purple and swollen testicles, and one end of the wire had been inserted into his urethra. The gaunt figure might have been dead but for an occasional twitching of his right ankle, which only served to make the vision that much more grotesque.

    Corbin remained pressed against that wall for all of five minutes before he found the courage to hazard another glance into the candle-lit room. Klein was still sitting in a lotus position, and Riddle had scarcely moved. At last, Corbin began to lightly tiptoe past the doorway. He kept his eyes fixed on the two creatures, ever fearful that Riddle would let out an alarmed cry or that Klein's head would swivel around like that of an owl. Neither of these fears were realized, however, and once he had made it past them, he broke into a stride that was as close to a run as he dared, desperately putting distance between himself and the room.

A metal, spiral stairway came into view ahead. Corbin further quickened his pace, anxious to take refuge in the darkness that it offered. Upon reaching it, he saw that it ran both upward and downward as far as he could see. The metal grating out of which it had been constructed was rusty and sharp and was considerably more painful to walk on than the previous stairway had been, but Corbin hastened to descend it nonetheless.

As he was approaching the third landing, he heard the unmistakable chitter of a malignant echoing through the stairwell, and he froze. He listened intently, trying to discern whether the sound had come from above him or from below, but the sound had ceased.

Corbin stood still, the metal grating digging into the ball of his left foot. What if the creature was sitting at the next level, waiting for him? He thought about turning around and making a run for the first window he came across, but he did not dare leave the castle without his sphere, so he forced himself to continue downward to seek out the Chatelaine.

At the bottom of the stairway, he found himself standing in a hallway of mirror-smooth aluminum panels. There were three braziers full of smoldering embers hanging from the ceiling of the fifty-foot-long passageway, and their reddish glow danced across the metal surfaces with a wavering, hellish glare.

At the far end of the hall, mounted on the wall just below the ceiling, was a bronze sculpture of three conjoined dog heads. The stumps of six white candles burned feebly in the sculpture's hollow eye sockets, leaving trails of melted wax that ran down the hounds' faces until they formed long, dangling stalactites. Beneath the weeping sculpture was a large door made out of vertical boards bound together with iron bands, and Corbin had an uneasy feeling that whatever was on the other side of that door was waiting for him.

Chapter Twelve
Through Blood and Water

Corbin hesitated with his hand on the latch of the door, dreading to face whatever horror might be waiting for him on the other side.

There is no other way, he reminded himself. *Escape means nothing if you don't take your sphere with you.*

He raised the latch and pushed the heavy, reluctantly squealing door inward. A draft of painfully cold air struck Corbin in the face, and he felt a sting on the bottom of his foot as he set it down upon a layer of thick, hoary frost. The room was approximately fifteen feet wide by thirty feet deep, seemingly carved out of solid stone. Two wooden tables ran down almost the full length of the room on either side. Each table was adorned with about twenty black candles, their dim blue flames casting a wavering, icy glow over the room's sparkling walls.

In the shadows at the far end of the room, floating in the air with her toes a few inches above the ground, was the form of a woman in a lacy gown that looked rather like a wedding dress. The form was singing to herself, her voice as gentle and soothing as a trickle of water passing over a stone:

Nud silladnah,
D'lruw uthvuh d'neh uthlit.
Reef neh villee'w,
Loh sidliech uthlit.
Leer tonsiteh,
Peelsah tsaph rauey.
Meard alla steh,
Tra'h roineh wo'nuey.

Corbin found himself caught off guard by the form's delicate shape and gentle voice. After the hanging man's dire warnings, he had expected something much different. In hindsight, he was not sure exactly what he had expected, though images of giant spiders and Minotaur-like creatures came readily to mind. This unanticipated apparition of a lady in white momentarily disarmed him, and he ventured a few cautious steps toward it.

The floating figure began to rotate. Beneath a veil of lace that came down as far as its upper lip, the creature had a Cheshire grin that stretched from earlobe to earlobe. Through the veil, Corbin could make out that the creature had no eyes, its forehead curving downward, smooth and bulbous, all the way to the bridge of its nose. Corbin noticed that she had a hoop of rusted metal around her neck. Hanging from it were well over a hundred large keys, and in the very middle of this cluster, attached to the hoop by a chain of tarnished silver, was a single, smaller key with a rounded, somewhat triangular shaped head.

The key that unlocks the birdcages, he realized with a flash of renewed hope. *The key to retrieve my sphere!*

The Chatelaine's jaw opened unnaturally wide, and Corbin took a cautious step backward. A long tongue emerged from the creature's mouth and began to lash at the air like a whip, and then she flourished her eight-inch-long fingers at him and let out a dreadful scream.

Seized by panic, Corbin began to retreat backwards toward the door, but the Chatelaine soared after him and struck him across the ribs with the back of her icy hand. The blow lifted Corbin off of his feet and sent him crashing down onto the table on his left. He painfully rolled off of the table, setting himself down on his feet again. To his horror, he observed that the Chatelaine had placed herself between himself and the door. She spread out her arms as if to offer an embrace, drew her tongue back into her jagged maw, and let out a deafening shriek.

Coming down here had been a mistake, Corbin realized. She was going to kill him, and the next time he awoke in his cell, Klein would be waiting to extract a terrible vengeance. A single goal fixed itself in his mind: He had to get away from her. He had to get back to his cell.

The Chatelaine glided forward again, swiping at Corbin with her elongated fingers, and he dropped into a crouch and sprang past her legs. By the time he got back onto his feet, the phantom was already bearing down on him, and he reacted by throwing a wild punch with his right arm. The Chatelaine darted away, rising into the air until her head nearly touched the ceiling, and then she came swooping down at him.

Corbin ducked and sidestepped to the right, and as the Chatelaine rushed past him, he gave her torso a shove. She crashed into the table on his left, floundering about and sending half a dozen candles clattering to the floor, and then she swept into the space between Corbin and the door once more.

She glided forward and swiped at Corbin's face, and he stepped backward and threw another punch. The Chatelaine shot back to avoid the blow and then rushed forward again, smacking Corbin across the side of his face with the back of her left hand and then again with her right palm, blinding him and causing him to stagger. Corbin's ears were ringing and there was a taste of blood in his mouth. He felt the creature's left arm swipe across his chest with so much force that he stumbled sideways, smashing his hip against the edge of the table with a numbing impact.

Corbin was still trying to recover his sense of balance when he felt the creature's large hands clamp down upon his shoulders. Her fingers were incredibly cold, seeming to suck all warmth, feeling, and strength out of his body. The Chatelaine's mouth fell open, allowing a cascade of drool and mucus to come pouring out over her lower lip. Her serpentine tongue lashed out, darting between Corbin's teeth and plunging effortlessly down his throat.

He gagged on the frigid, slimy rope of flesh, and his core temperature began to plummet. His eyes rolled involuntarily backward and, as his mind began to drift into a deathly sleep, he thought he heard a soft, soothing voice inside his head:

Sleep now, child…. Still your mind…. Still your heart….

The words seemed almost alien to him, stripped down to little more than the basic meaning that they conveyed: they were an invitation to let go of his fears and allow himself to fall into sleep. As cold and lightheaded as he was, the prospect of allowing himself to drift off into the warm embrace of oblivion seemed almost inviting.

She is a servant of Klein! He clung to this thought, using the horror of it to push back against the weariness that was coursing through him. *If I sleep now, I will wake up back in my cell, and she'll have told Klein what I've done. When I wake up, he'll be waiting for me!*

Exercising the last of his will, Corbin bit down on the Chatelaine's tongue. She let out a dreadful howl and flew back from him, black fluid spewing out from between her lips. Corbin stuck his fingers into his mouth, took hold of the icy tongue, and began to draw it out of his throat. It was nearly three feet long and the end of it tasted of gastric acid. He doubled over and retched as the lengthy muscle dropped to the floor, and all the while the Chatelaine continued to flail and shriek and bleed out before him.

Driven by adrenaline and desperation, Corbin threw himself at the stricken wraith. He came up on her left side, grabbed a fistful of her hair and dropped to his knees, dragging her down to the floor with him. He dashed the side of her face against the icy stone floor, and then he grabbed her jaw with his free hand and gave her head an abrupt twist.

He felt a momentary increase in tension followed by a complete release. The sensation reminded him of when the key in a windup toy has been turned so tight that the spring breaks, and the release was accompanied by a muffled snap like the breaking of a branch wrapped in layers of cloth. The Chatelaine's shrieking and flailing stopped. A black pool of blood continued to form around her head, steaming in the frigid air and melting the frost around her as it poured out of her grinning face.

The heat of the moment having passed, Corbin began to fully succumb to the shock of what he had endured. His body quaked and his sight seemed to grow dim, and for a while, he could do nothing but rock back and forth on his knees and try to breathe past the acidic vomit that seemed to have become lodged in his throat. At length, after having taken such time to compose himself as he needed, he lifted the Chatelaine's head and withdrew the ring from around her neck.

This is it, he told himself, regarding the smaller key which hung by itself. *The one that unlocks the spheres.*

Corbin was still quaking when he left the icy chamber, and the keys clicked and jangled together with every step he took. He clutched the ring to his chest with both hands, hoping to minimize the sound as much as possible.

He crossed the hallway and climbed back up the stairs without incident. When he approached the room in which he had seen Klein and Riddle, he dreaded to think that they might still be there, but his dread turned to horror when he discovered that they had gone. That meant that they could be anywhere. They might be waiting for him back in his cell or right around the next corner. His own breath sounded deafening in his ears as he slowly escorted the weighty, treacherously clinking mass of keys toward the next stairway.

Corbin had started to climb the stone steps when he heard the sound of clicking and of pattering feet. Ahead of him, three of Klein's minions were rapidly descending the steps. Corbin turned around and fled, but no sooner had he exited the stairwell than he heard one of the creatures let out a screech. The other two malignants shrieked in reply, and Corbin did not doubt that his presence had been detected.

He threw himself flat against the wall next to the door of the cell containing the woman on the sawhorse and held his breath. The creatures—two males and one female—bounded out of the stairwell and into the hallway. They began to skulk about, chittering and sniffing at the air, passing back and forth mere feet away from Corbin.

After a few moments, they began to move farther down the hall, clucking and snuffling, taking one cautious step at a time. Corbin's chest was starting to ache for want of oxygen, but he dared not draw a breath while the malignants were so close. They crept away, a few yards at a time, hesitating between their advancements to cluck or to sniff at the air. Finally, fearing that he would pass out if he did not breathe, Corbin softly exhaled. No sooner had he started to suck in a lungful of cold, refreshing air than one of the males turned around with an alarmed hiss, its sightless eyes roving vaguely in Corbin's direction.

Corbin cut the inhalation short, but the malignants were already beginning to limp toward him, chittering and simultaneously swaying from side to side. Soon the nearest creature's face was a mere two feet away from his own, and it began to sniff at him and to growl in the back of its throat.

He knows, Corbin thought. *He can tell that the wall isn't as flat as it should be. I should run. I won't make it far, but I have to run!*

In spite of this realization, he remained pressed to the wall, immobilized by fear and indecision. At that moment, either through good fortune or in a deliberate attempt at intervention, the man being tormented by burrowing eels let out a particularly loud moan. The three creatures pounced toward the door of the man's cell and started to shriek and chitter at him as if trying to determine whether he might have been the source of the disturbance they had sensed.

    Corbin, taking advantage of this momentary distraction, lightly sprinted off of the wall and into the stairwell. He saw two more malignants rushing toward him from above and flattened his back against the wall. They skirted past him, oblivious, one of them barely brushing his knee with its elbow as it passed.

    No sooner had he reached the top of the stairs than he heard a dreadful chorus of shrieks coming from below, and a notion that was as dreadful as it was absolute took root in his mind:

    They've found her! They've found the Chatelaine!

    Over the next few minutes, Corbin encountered no less than twenty malignants. They came in small clusters of three or five at a time, bounding around corners so suddenly that Corbin scarcely had time to conceal himself, but they seemed to be so preoccupied with reaching their destination that not one of them picked up on his presence. Eventually, he made it back to the hanging man. Upon catching sight of Corbin and the stolen keys, the hanging man cried:

    "Don't linger here, you fool! Flee! Such mischief has never before been perpetrated in the house of Klein, and I dread to think what he will do to you if he catches you now!"

    Corbin continued onward toward his cell, as soft and silent as a shadow. As he approached, the six young prisoners he had spoken to earlier pressed themselves against the bars, speaking in excited whispers at the sight of the ring of keys.

    "Hush!" he hissed at them, appalled by the clamor that their collective whisperings amounted to.

    "Where are you going?" the teen in the undershirt demanded as Corbin walked past him.

    "I'm going after my sphere," Corbin whispered. "I'll be right back."

A small chorus of groans and mutterings of disgust rose from the line of cells, and Corbin nearly ran in his haste to make it back to his own. He slipped inside, swung the door shut behind himself and sprinted toward his birdcage. Taking the hanging man's warning about fragments going dormant and passing beyond the point of no return to heart, he took a moment to regard his sphere. To his relief, the ghostly mass inside it was fluttering about with as much vitality as ever.

He tried the small key and, to his immense relief, the door on the front of the metal cage swung outward. He was not quite sure what to do next. Should he simply reach inside the fleshy doll and tear the sphere out of its chest? He reached his hand into the cage, and no sooner had his fingers caressed the surface of the crystal globe than the homunculus let out a shrill, bird-like squawk:

RAAAW!

The cry was deafening. Corbin was certain that if there was even a single malignant left on that floor of the castle, it was sure to come and investigate. Desperately, he wrenched the entire doll out of the cage and cast it down upon the floor, but it continued to writhe and to scream:

RAAAW!... RAAAAAW!

Corbin raised his leg to stomp on the doll's head, but he was hesitant to bring his bare foot down upon the stone floor with any great amount of force. Instead, he picked the doll up by its short, greasy legs and swung it against the wall on his right. The leather helmet struck the wall with a heavy *whump,* and the doll's torso rebounded with a wet crunching sound. Corbin swung it against the wall again, and still again. Bits of bone clattered to the floor and one of the doll's legs came off in his hand, and at last its leathery head broke off and went flying across the room. His Sphere of Torment came loose as well, flying halfway across the cell and striking the back wall with a reverberating ring.

Corbin was certain that the malignants would be upon him at any moment. He threw the remains of the doll's torso back into the cage, set its leathery head down on top of it, and slammed the cage shut. He then retreated to the corner, sat down cross-legged upon the keyring, and tucked his Sphere of Torment into the crook of his right knee. Then he waited for the inevitable arrival of his captors, hoping against all hope that the shattered, lopsided remnants of his doll would appear satisfactory to the malignants' sonar.

The malignants did not come. He cautiously got to his feet and began to approach the cell door, the keys clutched in one hand and his sphere in the other, listening for the sounds of footsteps and chittering. It seemed as if the disturbance had gone undetected, though it made his stomach turn to think that all six of his companions were going to have to pull off the same feat. He toyed with the idea of taking the hanging man's advice and making a break for it on his own, but the idea did not sit well with him.

It's all of us, or none of us.

There was no heroism in his heart as he approached the teenage boy's cell. All he felt was a grudging sense of duty born of the understanding that he would regret it to his dying day if he failed to live up to his promise.

"Well done, kid!" the teenager said, eyeing the keyring with a hungry look in his eyes.

Corbin examined the lock on the teenager's door. The keyhole was larger than the one in his own door, but not as large as some of the keys on the ring. He began to try some of the more likely keys, one after another.

"Son of a bitch," the teenager growled, reaching through the bars and snatching the keys away from him. "Give me that!"

Corbin took a dejected step backward, and the teenager started sequentially attempting to force keys into the lock.

"The little one hanging by itself unlocks your birdcage," Corbin explained. "You'll need your sphere before you jump."

"Jump?" the teenager inquired without looking up.

Corbin did not elaborate. He had been wounded by the manner in which the teenager had snatched the keys out of his hands, and now he relished the sense of validation that came from knowing something that the teenager did not.

At last, one of the keys worked and the cell door swung inward. The teen ran back to his birdcage, unlocked it, and took hold of the wickerwork doll within. The homunculus barely had time to let out a muffled squawk before the boy had twisted its neck hard enough to nearly detach its head from its body, and then he tore the reddish-brown globe out of its chest with a sound like a sapling being torn out by the roots. Next, he hurried out into the hall toward the cell containing the chubby boy in the white briefs. This time, he started skipping over keys of unlikely sizes, trying the most probable ones first.

Corbin's eyes wandered to the cell containing the woman with the painted leather mask. She was reclining toward the back of the cell, barely visible in the shadows, her wet eyes gleaming at him out of the darkness.

"What about the others?" he asked, his eyes locked with hers.

"What, the old-timers?" the teen grunted. "Leave them! We can't save everyone."

Corbin lowered his eyes. A part of him felt that the teenager was right; there were hundreds of souls locked away in Klein's castle, and there was no way that they were going to save them all. Still, he would have liked to have saved the woman without a mouth whose eyes said so much. He would have liked to have saved the hanging man and even the blind man, in spite of their protests to the contrary. In any case, the keys were no longer in his grasp, and he did not have the heart to fight with the teenager about how many souls were enough.

"There ya go, Charlie," the teen said as the cell door swung open, and he ran inside to unlock the boy's birdcage. Charlie cautiously ventured out into the hallway, his perpetually pouty face regarding Corbin with equal measures of wonder and gratitude.

The boy in the red pajamas was released next, and the teen in the undershirt handed off the keys to him before hurrying back to dispatch Charlie's homunculus. The boy in red disappeared into his cell, returned a few moments later with his blue sphere, and moved on to the cell of the girl in the white T-shirt and gray shorts. He passed her the keys, and she ran toward her birdcage. Less than a minute later, she had unlocked her cell door and stepped out into the hallway, her dark brown eyes glistening beneath a mop of curly black hair, holding her red sphere in one hand.

The curly-haired girl unlocked the cell of the teenage girl in the white crop top, who snatched the keys out of her hand and ran to release the boy in the white pajamas. She gave him the keys and he disappeared into his cell, and before long, he returned with his lime green sphere and passed the keys back to her. She then ran into her own cell, emerging seconds later with her purple sphere in hand.

"You know the way out?" the boy in the white pajamas asked Corbin.

"Yes," Corbin said and began to lead the way. They had not gotten far before he heard the teen in the undershirt hiss:

"*Veronica!*"

Corbin stopped and turned around. He saw that the curly-haired girl was standing before the cell of the woman who had been immobilized with barbed wire, her face conveying dumbstruck horror. Farther down the hall, somewhere off in the distance, Corbin heard the unmistakable chittering of an approaching malignant.

"We have to go," the teen in the undershirt urged in a whisper.

The girl tore her gaze away from the woman in the cell, nodded, and ran to catch up with them. A minute later, they passed by the hanging man. Corbin did not stop to speak to him, but their eyes met for a brief moment. The hanging man had a sad smile on his face, like a father who disapproves of his son's choices but is nonetheless proud of him. Corbin gave the man a quick, grimacing nod.

Yeah, you told me not to bring them, he thought. *And I went and did it anyway. If we don't make it to that window, you'll get your chance to say "I told you so."*

Upon reaching the window, Corbin prepared to throw his sphere through it, but then he hesitated. A bit of himself was trapped inside the sphere, he remembered. Would he feel himself falling? He doubted it. He had not felt anything when his sphere had torn out of his homunculus's chest and went sailing across the room. What if, he pondered further, his sphere were to shatter on the rocks below?

That'd actually be a stroke of luck, he reminded himself. *That was the next step, wasn't it? Finding a way to destroy the spheres.*

At last, he held his sphere through the window at arm's length and dropped it. He felt nothing, even after a time by which he was certain that it must have reached the bottom. The others, perhaps without understanding why, all hastened to throw their spheres through the window as well.

"We have to jump," Corbin told them. "The fall will kill you, and you will wake up. After that, you must go back to sleep and recover your spheres as quickly as you can before those creatures realize we've gone."

His plan did not extend beyond that point.

After that, he thought, *I suppose we just run off into the woods and pray.*

Veronica, the curly-haired girl, was the first to go out through the window. She swung her legs out over the sill, hesitated for a few seconds, and then pushed herself off. The blonde in the crop top went next, followed closely by the boys in the white and red pajamas. The pouty-faced boy, Charlie, climbed onto the ledge and sat there for all of ten seconds, gazing down into the abyss below.

"You need a push?" the teen in the undershirt asked, sounding impatient but not unkind. Charlie shook his head vehemently, hesitated a moment longer, and then found the courage to let himself fall.

"You're next," the teen in the undershirt addressed Corbin. Corbin nodded, pulled himself up onto the ledge, and dangled his feet out over the deep void beneath him.

You'd think this would be easy by now, as many times as I've done it.

It had not gotten any easier. Every instinct told him to pull himself back inside, and it was only with after taking several deep breaths and mustering all of his nerve that he was able to push himself out into that empty darkness. His heart leaped into his throat once more, and the cold wind stung his eyes and howled in his ears. At length, he smacked the surface of the water, shattering his ribcage and breaking his back upon a submerged stone.

Corbin woke up in his bed. He immediately got to his feet and started pacing about his bedroom, trying to shake an uncomfortable feeling of pins and needles out of his arms and legs. After about five minutes of this, he forced himself to sit back down, and another minute later, he was able to lie down flat. It took him twenty more minutes to fall back to sleep, and when he did so, he awoke to the feeling of cold water filling his nostrils and pouring unhindered down his throat.

He sat up in a panic, choking and retching and spewing water out of his mouth. He found himself in the moat that encircled the massive stone castle, the peak of which, he now realized, towered a full twelve stories above him. He stared up at the castle in awe for a moment, fully comprehending the grandeur of its dimensions for the first time.

The moat itself was surrounded by a nine-foot-high, slanting cliff of glistening rock that looked as if it was going to be difficult to scale. In the faint red flicker of the hanging braziers, he made out the shapes of the teen in the white undershirt, the boy in the white pajamas, Charlie, and Veronica all wandering about, stooped over and frantically splashing through the shallow water.

Upon noticing Corbin, Charlie wailed:

"Help us! We've found my ball, but we're still looking for the others!"

These words filled Corbin's heart with terror. Little enough good it would do them if they made it out of the moat and left their spheres behind. The blind man and the hanging man had both made it clear that the Winterland was full of perils. If they left without their spheres, it would surely be only a matter of time before some manner of harm befell them, at which point their bodies would be remade practically on Klein's doorstep.

Corbin began to splash and flounder through the water, dashing his shins upon ridges and groping in sinkholes, falling at times and becoming fully submerged in his desperate bid to find his sphere.

After about five minutes of fruitless searching, he saw a flurry of specks like floating bits of ash converging on a peak of rock close to the castle wall. They compacted against each other until they took on a solid form, reshaping themselves into the body of the blonde girl in the crop top. She drew in a gasping breath and sat up, and Corbin could hear the boy in the white pajamas explaining the situation to her as he went on groping and wallowing.

A few minutes later, the boy in the red pajamas emerged from beneath the water, coughing and spluttering in much the same manner that Corbin had. The teenager in the undershirt explained the situation to him, after which the seven of them went on searching for the lost spheres.

Corbin suddenly recalled that he had not thrown his sphere; he had dropped it, allowing it fall straight down from the window. Looking up, he became dismayed once more. Which window had they jumped from? How far had he already moved throughout the course of his panicked searching?

"Got one!" the blonde-haired girl announced, holding up a glass sphere. Even in the dim light that the hanging braziers provided, there was no mistaking its dark green hue.

"It's mine!" Corbin cried greedily. The girl gave it a careless, underhanded toss toward him, and it bounced off of Corbin's wrist and fell into the water with a sickening *plop*. Corbin cursed and fumbled at it, chasing it down a submerged incline until he had finally seized it and clutched it to his chest.

The others were still splashing about. By the look of it, Charlie was still the only one aside from Corbin who was not empty-handed. A prolonged shriek came from above them and, looking up, Corbin saw one of Klein's creatures hanging its head out of a fifth-story window. It shrieked again, and then it withdrew from sight.

"Shit!" the teen in the undershirt exclaimed.

"We have to go," Veronica said, making an awkward dash through the water toward the cliff that surrounded the moat.

"We don't all have our spheres yet!" Charlie protested. Two hundred feet away on their right, as if in response to this objection, a twenty-foot-high plank of wood began to fall away from the castle wall. It was a drawbridge, and it was being slowly lowered by two chains.

"Here they come," the boy in the red pajamas muttered, abandoning the search.

Corbin ran, stumbled, and splashed toward the cliff, dashing his toes and lacerating the soles of his feet on submerged stones. The drawbridge was about a third of the way down when Corbin reached the base of the cliff, and a hurried glance showed him no less than a dozen of Klein's malignants crowded at the opening, waiting for the bridge to fall into place.

He began to climb, grasping the sphere in his left hand. The cliff was smooth and steep, and Corbin found that he had to inch his way up on his belly rather than relying on hand and footholds. He was about halfway up when he heard the drawbridge fall fully open with a dull crash, followed closely by the sound of stomping feet and a flurry of clucking noises as the creatures started to make their way across it.

Corbin hooked his elbow over the peak of the cliff and dragged himself up. On his right, the boy in the red pajamas was helping the boy in white over the edge. The others were well ahead of them, crossing a stony field and fleeing toward the tree line.

By the time Corbin had gotten to his feet, he saw that the malignants had crossed the bridge and were scrambling over the rocks, bearing down on them. Then a dark cloud burst out of a window close to the top of the castle, and Corbin could see the red glow of the braziers playing across the surfaces of hundreds of fluttering wings.

He started to run toward the forest of oaks. The malignants were less than a hundred feet away, and the Luna moths were rushing after them with the speed of birds of prey. A voice cried out:

"Help me! I can't keep up!"

Corbin looked back and saw that the boy in the white pajamas was limping on his right leg, evidently having injured himself somehow either in the climb or in the search. Mere seconds later, the moths were swarming all over the boy. They latched onto clothes, skin, and hair, swarmed beneath him and bore him up into the air. The boy screamed as tatters of his clothes and small pinches of his skin were torn away and sent raining down into the moat, rendering him naked and nearly completely flayed in a matter of seconds. The moths dropped the slick, bloody figure several times, and each time, they would swoop after him and bear him up again, slowly making their way back toward the castle.

"*Jordan!*" the blonde-haired girl cried. She was standing at the edge of the forest, her face twisted into a mask of horror and grief.

The malignants were about fifty feet away by then, swarming across the rocks with catlike agility, homed in on the six remaining escapees. Corbin started to run again, terrified by the realization that he had fallen to the rear of the pack. The blonde-haired girl turned and disappeared. By the time Corbin reached the tree line, she and all the others were long gone.

He ran, crushing rotten acorns underfoot and tripping over half-buried roots as he fled for his life. His legs were burning, and his heart was beating mercilessly against his chest. He could hear the crashing of feet and a nightmarish chorus of chitters and clucks directly behind him, closing in, getting closer and closer with each passing second.

They are going to take me.

There was no question in Corbin's mind. He was going to be seized, and the last thing he was going to do before he was captured was throw his sphere as far away as he could. Perhaps it would not be found, and he might be given another chance to take his life and be reborn outside of the castle walls. It was not a likely chance, but it was the only hope he had left. Then, a panic-stricken cry came from somewhere off to his right:

"They're right behind us!"

The sounds of Corbin's pursuers began to veer off and fade into the distance, drawn toward the source of that self-destructive cry. He was not sure who had given it utterance—the teen in the white undershirt, he thought, or maybe the boy in the red pajamas—but their recklessness had given him a chance, and he began to run with renewed determination.

The farther he went, the lower the ceiling of the cavern became and the more twisted and deformed the oak trees were. While this change made it necessary for Corbin to be wary of low-hanging branches and deformed trunks, it also meant that the hanging braziers came to be set closer to the ground, which granted him better visibility. He moved along at a decent jog, ducking and weaving until he felt that it was impossible for him to go on, and he allowed himself to slump to the ground against the base of a twisted trunk.

He had only been seated for a few seconds, drawing in harsh, rasping breaths and massaging his aching legs, when he became aware of a new sound: the hiss of voices; the scrabble of fingers on coarse bark; the crisp shuffling of wings. Ancient, bare-breasted feminine forms garbed in loincloths were perched among the tree branches, their waspish wings stirring in agitation as they came out of hiding and gazed upon Corbin, their lips drawn back to reveal sharp, glistening teeth.

Corbin did not like the way they seemed to be grinning at him, nor did he care for the manner in which each of them seemed to move a little closer every time he looked away. He pushed himself off of the tree trunk, back onto his feet, and broke into a forward-tilted, breakneck sprint.

He heard the fairies hissing and laughing overhead. Their wings buzzed and wood creaked as they hopped from treetop to treetop, pursuing him, seemingly working their way onto increasingly lower branches as if to intercept him. There was something else too—something with heavier footsteps that was stamping its way over the blanket of acorns behind him—that seemed to be following him, never gaining, yet never falling behind.

When he could truly go no further, he dropped to his knees and allowed himself to collapse face-first into the jagged, putrid acorns. He lay still, defeated. The fairies continued to stir, flitter, and scramble, hissing and muttering among themselves. Corbin glanced over his shoulder and saw that they were circling around him, keeping to the higher branches now, casting troubled glances backward in the direction of whatever was pursuing him across the forest floor.

Corbin forced himself back onto his feet and began to stumble forward, and the footsteps of his unseen pursuer continued to follow him in a series of intermittent, quick dashes. The fairies growled and whined, leaping and buzzing from branch to branch as if longing to lay hands on Corbin but fearing that something might leap into view at any moment. Corbin lurched onward, at times barely able to walk, at times finding the strength to run a few paces, until something seemed to take hold of his spine and tear him violently backward.

COMING SOON

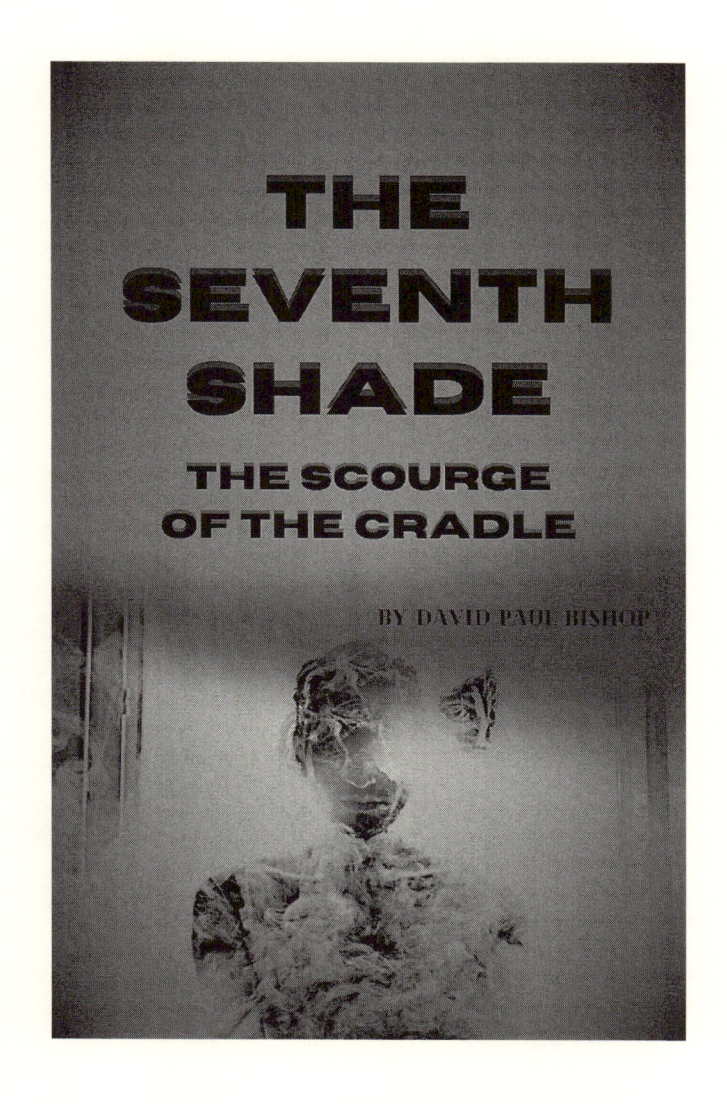

THE SEVENTH SHADE
THE SCOURGE OF THE CRADLE

BY DAVID PAUL BISHOP

Made in the USA
Middletown, DE
27 September 2022